SIX MILES SOUTH OF HAPPINESS

VICTORIA CONNELLY

Cover design by Jane Dixon Smith
Author photo © Roy Connelly

ISBN: 978-1-910522-27-1
Published by Cuthland Press.

To Timothy and Julia Blinko with love

'We must be willing to let go of the life we had planned so as to have the life that is waiting for us.' – Joseph Campbell

CHAPTER ONE

It was the biggest car boot sale in the area and Nuala and Paul Marshall had only ever been there as happy bargain hunters. Until now.

Now, the remnants of their possessions, collected over two lifetimes, lay spread before them on a double pitch. It was all the stuff that hadn't sold on eBay – the stuff that was too odd to take to the charity shop but too good to put in the bin. It was the stuff their friends or family hadn't wanted when pressed, the stuff you weren't able to recycle and the stuff they couldn't take with them into their new life on the road.

So much *stuff*!

Nuala looked at it all laid out before them and felt a twinge of guilt. The last few months had been a maelstrom of sorting and discarding everything they owned. She'd never thought of them as hoarders and their house had always been kept tidy, but it wasn't until you started opening wardrobes and drawers and wrenching suitcases and boxes down from loft and out from under beds and hallway cupboards that you realised just how many items had attached themselves to you over the years.

But they didn't want to keep it in an expensive storage unit and they couldn't take it all with them. So it had to go – all but the most basic essentials.

Nuala watched as a girl of about seven approached their pitch and picked up a teddy bear Nuala had had since childhood. It was in immaculate condition. Well, apart from the missing left ear. The girl stroked its yellow fur and, without batting an eye, handed a pound coin over to Nuala.

'It's three pounds,' Nuala told her, pointing to the label around its neck.

The girl just stared at her and Nuala sighed.

'Oh, all right then!'

The girl slipped back into the crowds and Nuala shook her head. Had the girl been taught that kind of cheek or was she born with it? A faint twinge of sadness filled her heart as she looked at the empty space on the rug which the bear had occupied. It was silly, really, to get so attached to inanimate objects and yet people did. People poured themselves into things, giving them far more meaning than they really had. Nuala and Paul had been reading books and watching vlogs about it all and internalising the messages. The magic of minimalism. The joy of decluttering. The power of letting things go. It had been so exciting to see the possibilities outside the confines of ownership.

Thinking of the progress they'd made over the last few months, she watched as pieces of their lives floated away before her eyes as, one by one, they were sold. There was the frying pan she'd inherited from a great uncle. It was a beautifully made thing, but just too heavy for everyday use. There was one of her favourite sets of novels being sold for a song. *Less* than a song! A fabric noticeboard she'd paid far too much money for. A four-foot plant they'd had for so many years that it felt like family. So many things holding so many memories.

She'd heard a piece of advice about photographing some of your possessions if you were having difficulty parting with them and she'd mulled it over for a while but ultimately decided that photos were just a different sort of clutter. They had digitised some of their most precious photos and Nuala had kept two photo albums: one of their wedding and another of favourite holiday pictures.

'Nu! I've just sold that box of cables for ten pounds!' Paul announced proudly, breaking into her thoughts.

'Really?' Nuala was impressed.

'There must have been something in there the man wanted.'

'I guess so.' Nuala grinned. That box of cables had been a point of contention for years. She'd tried to persuade Paul to get rid of it countless times, but he'd always remained adamant that they'd need something from it one day.

'We can buy...' he paused. 'What can you buy with ten pounds these days?'

'Not a lot,' Nuala said. 'But every penny helps at this stage.'

'Didn't our pitch here today cost twenty pounds?'

She nodded and laughed. 'And we've spent at least eight pounds on sandwiches and cake.'

Of course, there was also the money they'd spent on 'The Van'. Nuala still couldn't quite believe how much a modest-sized two-berth vehicle had cost them. Okay, so it had a toilet and shower and a tiny cooker and fridge. It wasn't exactly basic but, after having only ever lived in houses, it was going to take some adjustment. It had been a huge life decision, but one she was excited about. They'd leapt into early retirement after years of scrimping and saving, renting out their spare bedroom and making several income streams from setting up online courses while working their regular jobs. A small windfall from Nuala's favourite uncle when he'd died had been thrown into the pot as well. They'd paid for financial advice, making sure their pensions and investments were all in good shape before they took to the open road in search of freedom and adventure.

Nuala had to admit that she'd had some anxious moments as to whether they were making the right decision. To give everything up, to sell their home – it was pretty drastic. She'd seen the look of horror on her boss's face when she'd told her and she'd heard two of her work colleagues gossiping about her.

'She'll be back within a month,' one of them had said.

Nuala had smiled. She knew there was no going back. At fifty-five, she'd been dreaming about this for too long. She didn't want to spend another precious minute in an office, counting down the long years until she could retire and claim the state pension. She wanted to be in control of her own destiny – not be at the mercy of a large corporation and the government, telling her how long she should work and having them taking the best years of her life.

Paul felt the same way. He was the same age as her and he'd looked drained this last year. She was so glad that they had the same vision for a better, more exciting and healthier future together.

Saying goodbye to her job had been easy but leaving her home was going to be harder. Still, as much as she'd loved it over the years – the decorating of it, the choosing of colour schemes, the parties they'd thrown in it – it was just a series of rooms. And rooms trapped a person and tethered them to one place. When their great sort-out had begun, it had made her ask so many questions like why had she been buying so many things all these years? It was as if she'd been building a great wall around herself – a wall made of stuff. And now the wall was in the last throes of being dismantled. Some pieces were easy to let go of like the croquet set that had been a wedding present from a well-meaning relative who hadn't realised that they didn't have a large enough garden. It had sat in lofts and basements and garages over the years gathering dust and mould. Never opened. Never played with. But there were items that were hard to part with like the Christmas cactus she'd inherited from her grandfather. It was quite a size now and must be at least thirty years old and every single December, without fail, it would fling its fuchsia flowers into the world. But there was no room for it in The Van and so it had to go.

As the day wore on and they sold more and more of their items, she remembered the time they'd taken The Van out for a test weekend and how she'd loved the simplicity of it all. When had they allowed their lives to become so complicated? Why did people feel the need to gather so much clutter and chaos? She'd let her mind consider all the possibilities of the lives they hadn't chosen to live. If they'd bought a van in their forties – or thirties even – and lived simply, maybe they could have retired years ago. *Decades* ago. It had made her ask all sorts of questions about how society worked and how the school system seemed to be geared up to training compliant little worker bees who would stay put, pay their taxes and not complain. Young people seemed to be more clued-up on that today, she thought. The rise of the digital nomad and the number of people who were leading a 'Van Life' or living off-grid was increasing exponentially. It excited Nuala and, although she felt regret at the years she and Paul had spent trapped in jobs they had never really loved, she felt gratitude that they'd been able to get out now at least.

She glanced at Paul. He looked tired. More than that. It was as if the weight of what they were doing was finally dawning on him. She sidled up to him and put an arm round his shoulder.

'You okay?'

He nodded but didn't say anything. He wasn't much of a talker. Nuala tended to be the instigator in their relationship – the ideas person, the driving force. The Van had been her idea and it had taken more than a little persuasion before Paul had finally become excited by it.

'Shall we call it a day?' she asked. Most of the car boot crowd had gone and a few of the other sellers were leaving now.

They packed up the few items that nobody had wanted – even for ten pence. They'd just have to bin them, she guessed.

They drove home in silence. It had been an exhausting day. Nuala wondered how much they'd made. It must be a pretty decent amount even after accounting for the price of the pitch. She wondered if they could stretch to takeaway or if that would be too much of an indulgence.

As they pulled up to the house that was only going to be theirs for a couple more weeks, she glanced at Paul. He was looking at The Van that had taken over the driveway.

'Not long now,' Nuala said.

Paul gave a half-smile.

'Are you nervous?'

'Why would I be nervous?' he asked.

'I don't know. You look...'

'I'm just exhausted.'

They got out of the car and went inside and Nuala knew she couldn't be bothered rustling up anything nutritious in the kitchen and there wasn't even a table to eat it at now because they'd sold it. There was only the bed and a couple of chairs left in the entire house.

'Let's call out for pizza, shall we? Do you want to share a large one or shall we get two small ones?'

'I'm leaving.'

'What?'

'I'm leaving you, Nu.'

'But we're going to have pizza.' She frowned.

'You're not listening to me.'

'Yes I am. Where are you going?'

He was standing in front of her but he wasn't looking at her and something about the awkwardness of his body and the angles of it gave her a sudden chill.

'Paul?'

'I've met someone.'

'I don't understand.'

'I've met someone and I'm leaving you.'

'But...' her voice dried in her mouth. 'Paul!'

'I'm sorry. I should have said something. Weeks ago. Months ago!'

'*Months?*'

'I met her last year. I didn't think it was serious. But it was. It is.'

Nuala stared at him for a moment and then laughed. 'Oh, Paul! You had me there for a minute!'

'I'm not joking. I know I've handled this badly. But – well – I didn't know what to do. I kept putting off telling you because I didn't want to hurt you.'

There was something in his voice that sent a river of ice down her spine. 'You're serious, aren't you?'

'I'm sorry.'

There was a horribly long pause in which neither of them said anything.

'What's her name?' Nuala asked at last.

'You don't know her.'

'What's her *name*?'

'Saskia.'

Nuala nodded as if understanding perfectly.

'How old is she?'

'Nu! Don't!'

'Tell me!'

He sighed and ran a hand through his hair which had silver strands as well as chestnut these days. 'She's thirty-four.'

Nu swallowed hard. Twenty-one years younger than her.

Paul shook his head. 'No – thirty-two.'

Nu closed her eyes. Twenty-*three* years younger!

'How did you meet?'

'In the park. When I was jogging.'

Nuala sighed. She *knew* she should have gone jogging with him. He'd taken it up a couple of years ago as a way of getting fit after a minor health scare. At the time, Nuala had been glad to get him out of the house each Saturday and Sunday morning as it was easier to get chores done, but she should have gone with him. And then something else occurred to her.

'Is it because I went grey?' she said, her fingers combing

through her shoulder-length hair which, after much deliberation, she'd allowed to gently turn from blonde to grey. It hadn't been an easy decision. She'd been born blonde and then, since her early twenties, had topped up with highlights at least four times a year. But time and money and different priorities had convinced her that natural was better.

'It is, isn't it? You told me you didn't care what colour my hair was, but you do, don't you?'

'It's not about your hair, Nu!'

'But we're going away – it's all planned. *The Van!*'

'We'll have to sell it. I'm sorry.'

He said it so matter-of-factly. He truly had been thinking about this for weeks – or even months – hadn't he?

'But all those nights we spent talking about this! All those nights you let me dream! Did you *know* you weren't going through with it?'

'I... I wasn't sure.'

Nuala felt a flame of pure anger rising within her. 'So when *were* you sure, Paul? When you watched me accepting the offer on our house? When we sold the sofa? When I gave up my job?' She could hear the vile, bile-filled tone of her voice and she hated it.

'You can't blame me for any of this. You wanted to give up work and sell the house.'

'Yes, but with *you! Together!* This was *our* dream!'

He shook his head. 'No.'

'You said you wanted to see Europe.'

'I didn't.'

Nuala frowned. 'But we talked about it. We planned everything *together!*'

He looked at her then, his eyes full of emotion. 'It was your dream. Not mine. Never mine.'

Nuala felt her jaw drop as she tried to understand what he was saying. 'You didn't want to go?'

He shrugged. 'I would probably have gone. If I hadn't met—'

'Don't!' She couldn't bear to hear her name again.

He hung his head. 'You've always been the leader, Nu. You know that. And I've always been happy to follow.'

'Is *she* a leader?' Nuala asked now.

'No.'

His one-word answer seemed to say it all.

'How long have you hated me for?' Nuala whispered.

'I don't hate you. I could never hate you!'

'No? Well, guess what? I hate you!'

'Don't be like this.'

'How am I meant to be? You've just told me that our marriage is over and that the retirement we've been planning in detail for the last year is no longer happening!'

'Sit down,' he said gently.

'I can't.' She was pacing now. 'Is this some form of extreme decluttering – where you get rid of your wife?' she said with a bitter laugh.

'I really think you should sit down.'

'I sold my grandfather's Christmas cactus for £2.50!'

'Nu – come on.' He reached out and placed a hand on her shoulder, but she shrugged it off. 'It wouldn't have worked anyway.'

'What do you mean?' She stopped pacing and glared at him.

'I mean, we'd have got on each other's nerves. You're so – so controlling.'

'*What?*'

'We'd never have made it out of the UK.'

'How can you say that? We've been married for twenty-seven years!'

'I know. I'm sorry.'

'Paul!' she cried. 'I don't understand.'

Nuala felt like she was being sucked into some kind of void. What was he saying? Was he *really* leaving her? Were they *not* going travelling?

Paul seemed to sense her fragility and guided her gently towards one of the chairs that remained in the house.

'Come on. Sit down.'

'We're not going?' she asked. Her voice small now.

'No.'

She shook her head. Of course they weren't. So where was she expected to go? The house was being sold. They had to move out. Well, it seemed Paul had somewhere to move into at least.

'What am I meant to do?'

He replied, but she wasn't really listening now. She just felt numb. He was saying something about the house and The Van and the plans they'd made – the financial implications of separating.

She shook her head. It was all too much. Everything they'd ever done was so tied up in each other. She felt panicky at the thought of it all unravelling.

'You can't do this!' she said, hating herself for feeling so helpless.

He sighed. 'You'll be okay,' he told her.

'But I need you, Paul!'

'No. You don't need me. You never did.'

She watched as he picked up his car keys and left the house. He was taking the car, she thought. It was the last thing they'd been going to sell. She didn't suppose he would sell it now.

As she watched him drive away, she realised that, although he'd have to deal with the stuff they hadn't been able to sell at the car boot, the money they'd made was also in the car.

She cursed. He wouldn't be halving that with her, would he? Should she get a lawyer? Were they getting divorced? Her head hurt. She just wanted to run away. Their dream of doing that had been a powerful one and she wasn't ready to let it go just yet.

She looked around at the almost empty house. The new owners would be moving in soon and somebody was going to pick up their bed before that, having bought it last week. The plan had been to sleep in The Van after that so she'd just have to do that until she could find somewhere to live. A few nights of use shouldn't depreciate its value too much, should it? And yet she knew it would. They'd paid a small fortune for the vehicle, but she knew the secondhand market – even for something that was essentially brand new – was brutal.

A strange swirling surge of anger mixed with fear coursed through her. What would happen next? Was she about to be homeless, jobless, husbandless and directionless? She'd known she could cope without a home and a job going forward in her new life, but she'd never once imagined it without Paul by her side. Would she be able to go back to her job now? Her heart ached at the mere thought. But the real ache came from the death of her dreams. All those adventures she'd imagined for them both. The places they'd see and the fun they'd have. The mountains they'd climb and the seas they'd swim in. The joy, the laughter, the *freedom!*

All gone.
She'd never felt so utterly heartbroken in her life.

CHAPTER TWO

There was a young man flirting with her. She was quite sure of it. A very handsome young man too, she thought, as she began to flirt back. She gave a little flick of her hair and the smallest of smiles. Gosh, she hadn't flirted for years. It was a wonder she still knew how to do it, and yet she did and it felt good. A little bubble of excitement grew inside her as the young man smiled again. She liked this game. A game of smiles. A gentle appreciation of one another.

Sitting in the pretty café in the old town of San Sebastián on the Canarian island of La Gomera, she suddenly wished that she'd ordered a cocktail or a glass of wine instead of the rather unsophisticated fruit smoothie she was now struggling to get through. It probably made her look like a kid. But maybe that was the attraction? Maybe the choice of drink had knocked a few years off her. Perhaps she could market the idea as the fastest way to rolling back the years. Not that she was exactly ancient at fifty-two.

The young man got up from his seat and strode oh-so-confidently towards her table just as the straw made the rudest noise at the bottom of her glass as she finished the smoothie. He grinned and she could feel herself blushing. She'd forgotten how delicious that felt too – to blush when you felt somebody looking at you. *Really* looking at you.

'*Hola!* I'm Santiago,' he said. 'But you can call me Santi.' He motioned to the empty seat at her table and she nodded.

'I'm Laurie.'

'*Hola* Laurie. *Encantado.*'

He reached across the table and they shook hands. His was sun-warmed and olive-toned.

'You're Spanish?' she asked.

'Spanish. Some Italian too.' He gave a shrug. 'These things are just labels, aren't they?'

'I guess,' Laurie said. 'I'm English.'

His dark eyes twinkled. 'Of course.'

She blushed again. What had given her away, she wondered. Her accent or her horribly waxy white skin?

'You English like the sunshine here, *si?*'

She smiled. '*Si!*'

'And how do you like La Gomera?' he asked, gesturing around the square as if he owned it. Perhaps he did. Perhaps he was some Spanish prince and owned the whole island. He had a regal sort of look about him – that European glamorous look that *Hello!* Magazine adored.

'Oh, it's beautiful! I love it! So different from Tenerife.'

'I'm just here for the day. How long are you staying?'

She glanced at her watch. 'Until the evening ferry. I'm with a tour group. I have to rejoin them in twenty minutes.'

'So where are you based?'

'Los Cristianos.'

He grimaced and said something in Spanish that she didn't understand, but it didn't sound complimentary.

'*Why* are you staying there, Laurie? It's not the real Tenerife!' He sounded genuinely upset.

'Well, I was at a yoga retreat up in the hills for a week. But I needed to stay somewhere handier for everything after that. Somewhere I can take boat trips and book excursions from. I'm on my own, you see,' she confessed and then wondered if she'd done the right thing by telling him that.

He nodded and grinned as if he'd just won a small prize.

'And how are you enjoying your tour here?'

Laurie hesitated before replying. She was the only solo traveller on the coach and had been sat with a family of three from Italy. The husband, whom she'd been sat next to, was enormous and had manspread right across Laurie's seat. He'd also been monopolising the window seat instead of sitting by the aisle, which would have been a much better fit for his manspreading legs. And he'd insisted on talking right across Laurie to his wife and daughter on the opposite side of the coach.

'It's a good way to see the island,' she said diplomatically.

'I have a better way,' Santi said, motioning towards a motorbike.

Laurie looked to where it was parked. 'Oh, that must be fun!'

'It's the best! The sun on your face. The wind in your hair.'

Laurie smiled. The only wind she'd experienced on the coach was from the manspreader shortly after their lunch break.

'Come with me!' Santi suddenly said.

'What?'

'Forget your boring coach tour. I'll give you a tour of the island.'

'I can't just abandon my group!'

'Why not? You're a grown woman,' he said and she was quite sure he gave her entire body an appreciative glance. 'You can do what you want.'

'But I don't know you!' she said with a laugh at his boldness.

'What do you want to know? I'm Santi. I am a citizen of the world. I travel. I make my own way. I like food and bikes and beautiful women from England.'

She laughed.

'My mama says I am an adventurer,' he went on. 'My sisters say I should settle down and get married.' He shrugged. 'I don't like to be told what to do. I don't like tour groups or tourist traps. I like to see a place – *really* see it! And I want to share that with you, Laurie. Come with me! I get you back for the ferry. But don't go with the tour group.'

Laurie bit her lip. The thought of getting back on the coach squashed next to the manspreader wasn't an appealing one. She glanced across at the bike and then looked at Santi.

'I have two helmets.'

'Why?' she asked, suddenly suspicious.

'Because it's safer for making friends, right? And travelling with friends is more fun than alone, *si*?'

Oh, that smile of his! And those dark eyes twinkling as the sun filtered through the laurel tree shading them.

She started fiddling with her hair. She'd had her auburn locks highlighted just before coming away. It was an endless battle with the grey these days and she wasn't ready to go natural as some of her friends had. It was just – well – there was already too much grey in life, wasn't there? The British skies, the endless commute into work on grey roads, the office décor – it was all so grey. Laurie sometimes thought that her very insides must be grey by now and, if she died and they opened her up on the autopsy table, they'd declare 'Death by Greyness'.

Perhaps that's why she'd flown straight to the Canary Islands as soon as she could. She'd longed for sunshine. And adventure. And here it was – the chance to have an adventure and escape the greyness of life even if it was only for a few hours.

Hang on a minute, she thought, just as she was leaning into temptation – I'm a married woman in my fifties. *Should I even be contemplating getting on a bike with a handsome young Spaniard I've only just met? What would my husband say? What would my children say? What would the neighbours say?*

Laurie chided herself. She and her husband had most definitely been living in separate worlds even if they were still co-habiting. Her children had flown the nest long ago and probably wouldn't mind anyway, and Laurie had never really cared what neighbours thought. But what did *she* think? Was this a sensible thing to do? What if Santi was a reckless rider and they ended up going off a cliff? The roads on La Gomera were not for the fainthearted and she'd already seen the plunges down to the sea from the coach. Or what if he was planning to rob her? Or murder her. Or... She shook her head. She watched far too many Netflix documentaries. Besides, he didn't look like the dangerous kind. As far as she could tell. He looked kind. Fun-loving. Spontaneous. Life-affirming. Wasn't that just what she was looking for?

Santi glanced up at the sky. 'The sun won't smile forever, Laurie,' he told her as he kicked one of his biker boots against the other. He was ready to leave. 'Are you coming with me?'

CHAPTER THREE

Attrition. That's what it was – the slow wearing down of things: mind, body, spirit. It happened so slowly, with little bits of you getting chipped away in daily life, that many people didn't realise until it was too late. By then, you were so worn down that there really wasn't anything left of you at all.

That's how Elise Cherrington was feeling as she pulled up outside the small terraced house on the outskirts of the town where she'd lived her whole life: from primary school through to secondary and sixth form, this town had been her home. She'd escaped for three blissful years while studying art history in Edinburgh and she'd never forget that first train ride with her two small suitcases and backpack. It had been just a little bit too far and too expensive a journey for her to make regular trips home at weekends and she'd contrived to get seasonal work during the holidays, renting cheap rooms on the outskirts of the city. She'd planned never to return to the Midlands, but fate had somehow dragged her back.

Three long decades later and she was still here. Those

student dreams about working her way around Italy and renting a place in Venice or Rome seemed as distant to her as the places themselves. Of course, there had been that time she'd booked a tiny apartment in Florence for two weeks one spring after saving up for her thirtieth birthday. It had been the first holiday she'd taken out of the UK and she'd been looking forward to it for so long, imagining early morning strolls along the Arno, photographing the Ponte Vecchio before the tourists swarmed onto it and sitting – Lucy Honeychurch-like – under the Loggia della Signoria. But she had only managed the morning stroll because her mother's neighbour had called. Her mother had 'had an accident' and Elise needed to come back home immediately.

Elise still regretted having been manipulated like that. She'd packed her bags instantly and arranged her flight, paying a small fortune for a last-minute ticket and forgoing all but one night in the apartment she'd paid for. Her mother's 'accident' had been nothing more than a stumble and fall. There hadn't been so much as a bruise let alone a break.

Elise should have put her foot down after that incident, but that was easier said than done. Her mother had a way of controlling her – of layering familial responsibility with a truckload of guilt. And there was nobody else to share the burden with. Her older brother Michael had done the most sensible thing a child of Marie Cherrington could do – he'd emigrated to Australia and had insisted that neither his wage nor his job allowed for journeys back to the UK. While Elise occasionally cursed him, she also admired him and wished she had the courage and the means to make such an escape. She still dreamed of that Florentine apartment and the adventures she might have had if she'd stayed there for that precious holiday or had had the determination to take off to Italy as soon as she'd graduated. *The Other Life*, she referred to it as. An alternative Elise who had travelled the whole of Europe by the time she was thirty, seeing every piece of fabulous art and marvelling at the architecture before finally settling in a fabulous Tuscan town. She'd be fluent in Italian now and maybe even have a job in one of those famous Florentine galleries. She'd drive a vintage Alfa Romeo to all the hilltop villages but keep a Vespa for city travel.

This alternative Elise would drink the best wines and know all the best places to eat. She'd be welcomed warmly everywhere she went – in each little *ristorante* and *trattoria*. She might be the English lady with the crazy red hair and pale skin, but she'd be an honorary Italian.

Sitting in her bulky old Volvo now, which was about as far away from the spirit of an Alfa Romeo as you could get, Elise sighed. It had been a long day and her eyes felt gritty with tiredness – something she knew would probably be commented upon by her mother. She reached into her handbag and pulled out a lipstick to try and cheer her face up a bit. *Hibiscus Kiss*. She smiled. Somewhere, somebody had sat at a desk and come up with that name. Was that a fun job? Sometimes Elise couldn't help wondering if she'd taken a wrong turn in life and if somebody else was living her life – her best life. Maybe she should have been a lipstick namer or... or a horticulturalist, she thought fancifully. Maybe she would be leading a great life by now if she'd just applied for a different job. But what was a great life? Maybe some people were meant to just lead a quiet, dull life. Not that her life was dull.

Elise had chosen to go into conservation and had taken the role of custodian at Bevington House. The eighteenth-century mansion set in extensive grounds was about as fine a workplace as any you could hope for and Elise adored her office with its period ceiling and grand windows with views across the lake. She'd been overseeing the care of the house's collection of paintings, porcelain, furniture and textiles for over twenty years now.

The house had hit the news in recent years when, along with a number of other stately homes nationwide, it was revealed that it had been built from profits made from the sugar trade. It was hard to comprehend how these beloved tourist attractions could be given the name of 'Treasure Houses' when they'd been built on cruelty and exploitation.

Elise had known about the house's history when she'd taken the job on but hadn't really thought about it until it had been placed in the full glare of public scrutiny. There'd been no hiding from the spotlight shone in their direction and she had to admit that she couldn't look at the collection objectively anymore. Each piece she handled and cared for was affected by its past. How many lives had paid for that Gainsborough portrait or those Chippendale chairs, she'd wonder? How much suffering had been caused so these fine plaster ceilings and acres of gleaming glass could be purchased? How much had the original owners been aware of all that? Had the women of the house been sheltered from the whole thing? So many difficult questions were now being asked.

The truth was, Elise had loved her job for many years, but there'd still been that sense that something was missing. After all, a good job didn't love you back and, when she left Bevington House at the end of each working day to return to her own humble house on the outskirts of town, she couldn't help feeling that there must be more to life. Bevington was beautiful, but it was just a house and her life there was so sheltered, so *local*, and her days rarely varied. The most exciting things to happen were the seasonal fairs throughout the year or when there were school visits. She smiled as she remembered the time a thirteen-year-old boy had broken away from his classmates and found his way to her private office.

'I'm bored,' he'd told her.

Elise had been startled but then amused and had taken him under her wing, giving him a tour of some of the private rooms and telling him some of the saucier stories from history that his teacher had managed to avoid. When she'd returned him to his party, she'd thought about the interaction for a long time – the buzz she'd felt. Most of her days were spent alone behind closed doors. She'd sometimes receive visiting historians and fellow conservators, and she liaised with the owners to curate special exhibitions for the public, but it was essentially a solitary post.

Putting thoughts of work aside, she got out of her car and fixed a smile on her face that felt uncomfortably at odds with how she was feeling as she walked to the front door.

'It's just me, Mum!' she called through after letting herself in with her key. She didn't need to ask her where her mother was. She'd be in 'The Chair'.

At eighty-one, Marie Cherrington struggled to do pretty much everything except complain. Horribly overweight with more diet-induced issues than you could shake a celery stick at, she berated the world for her misfortune. And yet she had done nothing to combat what Elise could clearly see were self-inflicted conditions. A good wholefood diet, regular exercise and a positive attitude could have gone a long way to reversing so many of her mother's issues over the years, but she'd have none of it. It was as if she'd claimed The Chair as some kind of weird prize where she could sit commanding others to do her bidding.

Elise removed her shoes and checked her reflection in the hallway mirror even though she'd just checked it in the car. She liked this mirror. It had belonged to one of her grandparents and its mottled surface was gorgeously flattering to a face that was struggling with menopause-induced insomnia and general lethargy.

'Where are you?' her mother called through from The Chair.

'I'm here, Mum.' Elise walked through to the front room and grimaced at how dark it felt. It wasn't just because her mother kept the curtains half-drawn. The old brown sofa, the dark wooden shelves and the ancient carpet all did their best to suck out the light on even the brightest of summer days.

'You don't look well. What's wrong with you?' her mother snapped. The question was asked not to determine what was actually wrong with Elise and to show sympathy for her, but more as a disgruntled reaction to her having brought her woes into her mother's living room.

'Nothing's wrong with me,' Elise assured her.

'Your eyes are red and you've got blotches on your face.'

Elise's hands flew automatically to her face even though she'd been looking at it just seconds before and knew, for certain, there were no blotches there. Her *Hibiscus Kiss* lipstick hadn't been enough of a distraction, Elise thought.

'I've had a terrible day,' her mother went on. 'You wouldn't believe it.'

'I'm sure I would,' Elise whispered under her breath as she picked up the local newspaper which had been thrown on the floor. Just once, wouldn't it be marvellous if her mother could welcome her with a warm smile and a happy greeting? Maybe even ask her about the day she'd had. Show an interest. *Care.* Instead, Elise was subjected to a seemingly endless list of all that was wrong with the world and how it had managed to find its way into number thirty-eight and right to The Chair.

Elise honestly thought that her mum spent her days banking up all her complaints – maybe even writing them down in a notebook and memorising them – before unleashing them on Elise. Had she never heard of the practice of writing down all that you're *grateful* for? Maybe Elise should suggest that although she could virtually hear the scoffing response she'd get.

'Mum, you shouldn't be worrying about all this,' she tried instead.

'What do you mean?'

'I mean, it doesn't do you any good. So there are roadworks at the end of the road. It doesn't really affect you, does it? You couldn't hear them, could you?'

'They're always digging this road up!'

'No, they're really not. And the lunchtime rain surely didn't affect you.'

'Colleen's coat was dripping wet when she arrived!' her mother pointed out. Colleen was the latest in a long line of cleaners that Elise had arranged for her mother. The previous one had refused to come anymore after Marie Cherrington had thrown a cushion at her.

'She said she'd plumped it and she hadn't,' her mother had told her. 'I said, "Does that feel plump to you?"'

'And I'm sure your lasagna was just fine,' Elise went on, doing her best to try and change a personality that was so entrenched after eighty-one years that there was very little hope for it really.

'*You* didn't have to eat that dried-up dish!' her mother continued undeterred. 'Like soggy cardboard!'

Elise frowned. How could something be both dried-up and soggy? Either her mother was getting dementia or she was just telling lies and not able to keep her story straight. Elise suspected the latter. With her mother, it was always drama for drama's sake. A very nasty case of the ego demanding attention and not caring if it was positive or negative. Attention was attention.

'Can I make you a cup of tea before I go?' Elise asked.

'Where've you got to go to?'

Elise paused before answering, not wanting to reveal that she had nothing whatsoever planned for her evening because her mother would keep her trapped at number thirty-eight if she knew that.

'I'm seeing Jasper.'

Her mother harrumphed. 'Ridiculous name.'

Elise cleared her throat. It was, indeed, a ridiculous name for her to have come up with. She wasn't totally sure where it had come from. She'd never known any Jaspers and yet it had just popped out that evening when her mother had dared to suggest that Elise move in with her.

'You'll never marry now,' she'd told her with some delight. In that one moment, Elise had seen the dreadful trajectory her life could take if she allowed her mother to rule it. The long, lonely days at work followed by the torturous evenings with her mother. She'd known she needed a way out.

'Actually, I'm seeing somebody,' she'd blurted.

'Who?'

'You don't know him.'

'Is he living with you?'

Elise had paused before answering because the man in question didn't actually exist. Well, he sort of did – in her mind. Especially on evenings when Netflix or a good book in a warm bath just weren't enough to combat the loneliness. Then she'd dream. She'd dream of meeting someone who would be both strange and yet familiar: strange in that he'd be so completely outside her own tiny realm that he'd colour her dull life with wonder, and yet familiar in that way of when you meet someone and instantly feel that you've known them all your life.

'He doesn't live with me, but he comes over a lot,' she'd explained.

'But he won't marry you? Is that it?'

'Mum!' Elise could see the malicious mischief in her mother's eyes.

She'd asked to see a photo of him and Elise, not wanting to sow suspicion in her mother's mind, had pulled out her phone and scrolled. How hard could it be to find a suitable photo? Unfortunately, the only recent ones from work were of her and a visiting historian whose work she admired, but he was old and overweight and wouldn't do at all. So she quickly went online and searched for Tom Hiddleston, trying to choose a photo of him that wasn't a red-carpet moment and that definitely wasn't him as a Marvel hero. She should be able to get away with it as her mother didn't watch a lot of films.

When she'd presented the picture to her, Marie had given a strange sort of snort, but hadn't said anything.

Elise had had to fight hard not to laugh out loud. Even her mother couldn't find fault with Tom Hiddleston.

Now, as she made her mother a cup of tea, she thought about Jasper and what – if he actually existed – they might do that evening. Perhaps they'd have a meal at a pub before heading home to snuggle up on the sofa to watch a film. It was such a simple, cosy image but it filled Elise with sadness when faced with the reality of her evening – alone with a book.

She'd had partners, of course. Few people made it into their fifties without having been spun on the romance merry-go-round a few times. But nothing had lasted beyond a couple of years. Elise had often wondered if it was some fault in her. Her mother seemed to think so and was sure to tell her as each relationship ended.

While she waited for the tea to brew, she frowned as she remembered the time her mother had told her she wasn't surprised to hear that Tim – whom she'd never met because Elise never brought her partners to meet her mother – had left her.

'He's obviously got better things to do than look at your miserable face all day.'

Weren't mothers naturally meant to be on the side of their daughters? Shouldn't Marie Cherrington have been dissing Tim and telling Elise that she'd had a narrow escape, even if she hadn't, because that's what mothers were meant to do?

Elise caught sight of her reflection in one of the glass-fronted kitchen cabinets. It *was* a miserable face, she had to admit. But she couldn't help feeling that there was something inside her – some little flicker of light that hadn't yet been extinguished and was just waiting for a time when it could be fanned into fullness.

She took the cup of tea in to her mother along with a

plate of biscuits. It probably wasn't a great idea to encourage her mother's sugar addiction, but she couldn't see that she was going to change her ways now.

'You're too old for long hair,' her mother said out of nowhere as she took a biscuit.

Elise just stared at her for a moment. Was there not *one* kind and caring bone in her body? Why couldn't she just say something nice?

There were times when Elise wondered if there was a reason her mother was the way she was – some incident in her childhood, perhaps? Or the way she'd been brought up. Maybe her parents had been the same and it was learned behaviour? Her mother would occasionally refer to her upbringing and it didn't sound easy with a tough father who'd once locked his daughter out of the house for coming home too late, and a mother who hadn't been able to handle money and was always getting into debt. That couldn't have been easy to be around as a youngster, Elise thought with kindness.

And there were times when her mother would fall asleep in The Chair. With her eyes closed, it was easy to imagine her as that innocent child, and to have compassion for whatever she'd been through. But, as soon as her eyes were open, the invective would begin again.

Sometimes, Elise wondered if it would be easier if her mother slipped into dementia. Would that do something to erase the nastiness? Or would it make it worse? It might mean she'd have to be in a home. Elise felt horribly guilty when she had such thoughts, but she just couldn't help it. It was a way of escaping the pain of the present moment – to imagine a gentler, kinder future for herself.

'I don't think a woman should have long hair after the age

of forty,' her mother went on. 'No. *Thirty.*' She nodded to herself, having set the world to rights with her uncompromising opinion. 'And yours has always been tricky hair, hasn't it? All those tight red curls just like your father's, God rest his soul. It's a wonder you still wear it like that.' She made a scoffing noise. 'A red mass of embarrassment.'

Elise's hands flew to her hair to try to flatten it. It was always a little frizzy in damp weather.

'I have to go... Jasper...'

'Yes – the mysterious Jasper!'

Elise swallowed, suddenly anxious that her mother was going to challenge her about his existence.

'When am I going to meet him?' she asked.

'I don't know. He has strange work hours at the moment and he's out of the country a lot.'

'What did you say he does?'

Elise glanced down at a watch she wasn't wearing. 'I have to go.'

As she got back in the car, she stared out of the window at the street she'd stared at for more years than she cared to remember. Her heart was racing and her head was pounding. She felt dreadful and she didn't know how to fix it. All she knew was that this feeling of dissatisfaction was wrong. You shouldn't dread each day, should you?

She was following a social media account – a woman in her thirties who travelled the world as a digital nomad. The photos were jewel-bright with backdrops of sun-kissed beaches, windswept mountains or lush green valleys. The woman sang beautifully, and she played the ukulele. Of course she did! Some days, it was hard not to hate her for the seemingly perfect life that she led and for all those golden moments she experienced.

Oh, to have golden moments, Elise thought as she started her car and drove home. Or at least one. Just *one* to counteract the many grey ones she endured. She felt she could survive if she had a golden moment to carry deep within her. Perhaps she should learn the ukulele. She tried to imagine playing one on a bench in her local park. She'd probably be set upon by the neighbourhood dogs.

In her heart, she knew that life for Ms Ukulele wasn't all dolphins and rainbows. She would occasionally post about the horrors of world travel – the rat-infested hotels, the streets full of rubbish and the endless hassles that came with travel days. But those posts were few and far between – Elise saw them as a kind of tax the YouTuber had to pay so as not to be universally hated by her followers for the otherwise wonderful life she got to live.

Later that evening, having binge-watched two episodes of a period drama while eating far too many chocolates, Elise stood in front of her bathroom mirror examining her hair. What had her mother called it?

A red mass of embarrassment.

Opening the bathroom cabinet, she took out a pair of scissors and grabbed a handful of her red curls, her eyes misting with fury. She looked at her reflection and the face that her mother had never shown any pride in or affection for. Then, biting her lip, she cut a chunk of the red curls, watching in fascinated horror as she dropped them into the sink below.

She exhaled, tears falling down her cheeks. That wasn't too hard, was it?

She looked at her reflection again and grabbed a second handful of hair.

It was then that her phone rang from the adjacent bedroom.

She put down the scissors and went to answer it.

'Is that Elise Cherrington?' a woman's voice asked.

'Yes it is.'

'My name's Dr Anna Hudson. I'm calling from Northampton General Hospital. I'm afraid I have some bad news for you. Your mother was admitted to the hospital after calling for an ambulance. And I'm afraid she died of a heart attack twenty minutes ago. I'm so sorry. There wasn't time to contact you before but I found your number in her phone. I really am sorry.'

Elise stood in her bedroom, frozen to the spot for a moment. The first thought to pop into her head was that she didn't need to cut her hair now, did she?

CHAPTER FOUR

The day after Paul had walked out of their marriage, Nuala woke up with a crashing headache. It wasn't really surprising. Her headaches were often nature's way of telling her to rest after a stressful situation.

A part of her wanted to bury her head under the pillow and sleep until the new owners turfed her out, but she knew there was too much to do and so got up, leaving the bed that she'd shared with Paul for almost thirty years.

And where was he waking up, she wondered? With *her*? With *Saskia*?

The name rolled around her mind for a moment. To her, it sounded snake-like and sinister. You couldn't possibly be sweet and kind with a name like that, could you? It was the name of someone manipulative – the sort to pick up somebody else's husband in a park in full daylight.

Nuala sighed. Such thinking wasn't going to fix things nor was it going to sort out the enormous amount that now had to be done. Where did you start, she wondered? Was there a manual or an online guide? Maybe somebody had made a YouTube video about it.

'*What to do when your husband leaves you on the eve of selling your house and when you've just given up your job to go travelling the world in a van together*'.

Hmm, maybe that wasn't the catchiest of titles, but she'd take a look on her laptop later.

She took a shower and got dressed. The large wardrobe they'd shared over the years was virtually empty now and she noticed that Paul had taken all his clothes. When had that happened and how hadn't she noticed? Had they been in the car or had he taken them to Saskia's before the car boot sale?

As she walked around the house, she noticed other things were missing too – his toiletries from the bathroom, his favourite mug from the kitchen and his jackets and trainers from the understairs cupboard.

Nuala swore colourfully, but it didn't make her feel any better.

She hadn't realised she'd been married to somebody so... what was the word she was looking for? *Stealthy*? That was a pretty good word. It amazed her how long he must have been planning this and her memory spiralled back in time as she tried to replay scenes from their recent interactions from his point of view. Like the time she'd been showing him a route through France she wanted to take.

'What do you think?' she'd asked, pointing out the section of coastline she wanted to see.

'Yes – whatever you want to do.'

Hadn't that been what he'd said? When he'd *known* that they weren't going? Why hadn't he told her? Why had he let her go on dreaming and planning for all those months? It was nothing short of cruelty – to let her visualise their future together and get excited about something that was never going to happen. She'd even bought a brand-new hardcover notebook with crisp white pages with perfect feint lines on which she'd written, in her best handwriting, lists of cities and museums, of national parks and rivers, of mountains and forests that she'd hoped they'd be able to see. She felt so angry with him about that – maybe more so than his having fallen in love with somebody else because she guessed you couldn't actually help that. In a way, she kind of understood him, but she couldn't understand somebody who would lie and plot and cheat.

He'd said she was controlling. Was she? She'd always considered herself the leader in their marriage – the driving force. There wasn't a single house move or renovation that hadn't been her idea. But that wasn't being controlling, was it? That was just being organised. The same with the goals they'd striven towards – whether it had been saving for a special holiday, buying a new car or planning for their early retirement. These things needed to be coordinated. You had to have at least one of you in a marriage who knew what was going on. Things didn't just happen on their own. And Nuala had prided herself on being passionate and driven. She'd always been excited by her vision for them and, until Paul had dropped his bombshell, she'd thought he had been on board with them both taking early retirement and travelling.

But he hadn't, had he? Or maybe he had? Maybe there'd been a turning point, but when? When had he decided he wanted out? Was it before or after he'd met Saskia? If he hadn't met her jogging in the park, would he have still gone along with their road trip plans? He'd told her it wouldn't have worked out between them even if he hadn't met Saskia.

So maybe he had been planning on leaving her before they'd set off.

She shook her head. She was torturing herself with so many questions and she knew it wasn't likely that any of them would be answered because Paul wasn't replying to her calls or texts and she'd left quite a few messages for him now.

As she walked into the kitchen and idly opened a cupboard for food, she wondered what her options were now and if she should try and reverse as much as she could. She couldn't stop the sale of the house, but maybe she could get back some of the stuff they'd sold and given away. She frowned. Just how was she going to do that – go into the charity shops, tell them her sob story and hope she'd get back the old sideboard and cutlery sets she'd happily donated? Then she'd have to find a place to rent and find the money to pay that rent which would probably mean getting her job back which was the very last thing she wanted to do. She could just imagine the smug look on some of her colleagues' faces if she dared to return to the office.

'Well, it was a nice dream to have,' Angie on reception might tell her, 'but not very practical, right?'

Nuala winced. She didn't want to be told that. She didn't want people to think that her dream had failed because she knew it was a good dream. Better than that – it was a *fantastic* dream and she knew she could have made it work because she'd been on the cusp of making it happen. But a vital component of it was now missing and the whole thing seemed to be falling apart.

Anyway, even if all the practicalities in the world told her she should go back to her job, she knew she couldn't. She felt the same way about trying to retrieve all the stuff they'd sold and given away. She didn't want it all back. She didn't want *any* of it back. Something had shifted inside her and she knew that the only way was forward. Her work colleagues were most definitely *ex*-work colleagues. The only thing she'd ever had in common with them was the time they'd shared together as office workers. They'd never understood her dream of travel.

Nuala also knew that, at this point anyway, she didn't want to talk to her family. Her parents would no doubt be relieved and her sister would tell her it was probably all for the best.

As she took a couple of painkillers and rejected the idea of a bowl of muesli, she acknowledged the fact that she was truly on her own with what she did next.

She walked into the living room and looked out onto the driveway where The Van was parked. How beautiful it looked – a true dream machine that she'd never drive now. She wouldn't get to see those picturesque Loire Valley roads or climb those alpine slopes or venture across the plains of Spain. She wouldn't ever know what it felt like to wake up to a view you'd chosen to wake up to and to fling the door open and step out into a brand-new day in a brand-new place. She would never know that freedom that she'd dreamed of for so long.

Unless...

A tiny tickle of an idea began to form.

Unless...

She looked at The Van with desire in her eyes and her dream still very much alive in her heart.

Just go!

The little voice inside her sounded so faint that she could barely hear it. But hear it she did.

Go. Go now!

She shook her head. She couldn't. They had to sell The Van. They were separating and very likely divorcing and that cost money, didn't it? Everything would have to be split including the money from The Van.

But he's got the car.

The rebel voice was getting louder now.

He's got the car and he's the one who walked out on you.

Nuala continued to stare at The Van – the beautiful dream machine that she'd poured everything into over the last few months of her life – and she knew she couldn't sell it. She just couldn't.

Go. Go now!

The little voice inside her was louder still. And she knew she couldn't ignore it.

CHAPTER FIVE

Had somebody told Laurie Graham that, just two months from now, she'd be sitting outside a sunny café on the island of La Gomera flirting with a man three decades her junior, it might have raised a wry smile – a chuckle even. She certainly wouldn't have believed it. As much as she'd have wanted to.

But, on that dull grey day in the dull grey office at work, she really wasn't in the mood for humour.

'Yeah, yeah!' she might have said. 'Now, what are we going to do about the double-booked meeting room this afternoon?'

Ever since she could remember, Laurie had wanted to travel. As a child, she'd been mesmerised by the alpine beauty of *The Sound of Music*, desperate to twirl and sing in the middle of the mountains like her heroine Maria von Trapp. Then, as a teenager, she'd fallen in love with the Africa of *Born Free* and imagined herself raising abandoned lion cubs. Adolescence had supplanted the lion Elsa with Robert Redford from *Out of Africa* and she envisioned romantic moments involving shampoo and poetry.

But then life had happened and those dreams of seeing the beautiful places of the world had slowly drifted away – or rather they'd been wrenched away and placed behind a paywall that her meagre salary couldn't ever seem to chip away at. She hadn't even had the chance to travel much as a child because her mother suffered from motion sickness and her father had never trusted his beloved Jack Russells to anyone else. Even the school trip to France had been cancelled because bad weather meant the ferries weren't running.

She'd hoped for great things when she'd married Jeremy but, at ten years older than her, he'd already seen enough of the world through his job in sales. He didn't like venturing abroad. He liked the Cotswolds. And Wales. Laurie had seriously had enough of Wales over the years. It was so cold. So slatey. So *grey!* She longed for sunny climes and would often buy glossy magazines or order holiday brochures and casually leave them around the house, hoping Jeremy would take the hint. But he never had.

'Look at the price of that!' he'd scoff as he sliced the head off his boiled egg and covered the photo of Laurie's longed-for beach in toast crumbs.

'It would be warm,' she'd tell him. 'We could swim in the sea.'

'Oh, no, no, no! You'd get sunstroke within half an hour. No chance of that at Cardigan Bay, is there?'

'No,' Laurie said. 'None at all.'

Cardigan Bay! Even the name told you it wasn't the place for a bikini.

She'd lost count of the number of cold, wet holidays they'd had in the UK over the years while her friends and colleagues jetted off to the Mediterranean and the

Caribbean. She'd had to compliment them on their holiday glow when they came back while her limbs remained pasty white. But perhaps she'd get the last laugh about that now that the ageing process was catching up with them all and her skin – which hadn't seen much sun over the years – was remarkably wrinkle-free at fifty-two.

Of course, her fridge was covered in travel magnets – there was a windmill from Amsterdam, the Roman Colosseum, a palm tree from Florida and a flamenco dancer from Spain. Only she'd never seen any of those things because each and every one of those magnets was a gift from friends and family – people who *had* been to those places.

Laurie couldn't believe that there were so many places she hadn't seen – countries covered in jungle, desert and ice – all unseen. Rivers, mountains, canyons – all unseen. Dolphins, gorillas, elephants – all unseen. Her eyes were hungry to see it all and her heart ached to experience it.

Their only holiday abroad in the last five years had been to Tenerife, but Jeremy hadn't wanted to leave the all-inclusive resort.

'But don't you want to see the volcano?' Laurie had asked.

He'd given her a look as if she was quite mad.

She hadn't dared mention the paragliding she'd hoped to book for them.

Oh, how she'd longed to explore the island. She'd done her research and knew there was much more to it than the busy resorts, but she hadn't seen any of it because – and this was a tough admission – she was scared. Scared to go on her own. Scared she'd get lost. Scared to even book an excursion. How crazy was that? So she hadn't seen dolphins or pilot whales on a boat trip, she hadn't gone paragliding and she certainly hadn't climbed up the volcano.

'Think of the money we've saved,' Jeremy had boasted when they'd boarded the plane home having seen nothing. He hadn't wanted to spend more money than was absolutely necessary. Anything that wasn't included with the wristband that had been firmly attached on arrival was strictly prohibited.

Sometimes he'd try to placate her with promises of a bit of travel once they'd both retired, but she didn't believe him. And this mythical 'retirement' date seemed to be getting pushed back further and further every year by both her husband and the government. Together with the rising cost of living, it sometimes felt you could never have enough savings in the bank and things like luxury trips seemed completely unattainable, especially after you'd raised two children. But they were all just excuses. The truth was, Jeremy was a skinflint and set in his ways. Even if they were millionaires, he wouldn't touch a penny or treat them to a luxury holiday abroad. He would rather sit and count his money in the comfort of his own home rather than spending it in a foreign country creating wonderful new memories.

Laurie adored Tilly and Joseph. She'd always wanted to be a mother and hadn't ever cut corners when it came to spoiling them. They'd both left home now although Joseph did have a habit of dropping by for Sunday lunch, a big bag of washing in tow. Tilly occasionally rang up and would casually mention an unexpected bill that had just landed. Laurie knew she shouldn't always give in to them but it was hard to say no.

Still, she felt worn down by it all. Life sometimes seemed to be an endless cycle of work and paying bills. Whatever happened to play? When had life become so exhausting and unrewarding? And hadn't Jeremy promised that she could quit her job once the children had both left home? What had happened there? She should confront him about that for sure even though she knew what he'd say.

'Just another year or two.'

Well, the truth was, Laurie didn't want to wait another year or two. She'd lived her whole life waiting. She wanted to explore and have adventures *now* – to fling herself off a mountain and paraglide towards the sea, to swim off the back of a boat in water so clear and blue that it hurt your eyes to look at it. And she didn't want to be in her late sixties when she started to live life and travel. She was already experiencing the first twinges of arthritis in her left knee and years of inappropriate shoes had no doubt destroyed her feet. But she still had energy. Well, as long as she remembered to stick her HRT patches on twice a week.

The last time she'd mentioned her concerns about her waiting until her sixties to retire, Jeremy had told her she was being melodramatic.

'It's what people do,' he'd said.

He'd made her feel guilty for questioning the rules of society. But more people were taking early retirement these days, weren't they? She'd watched her fair share of YouTube vlogs about it, nodding in agreement when hearing the warnings about declining health as you got older. And what if something worse happened? What if you didn't actually make it to retirement? Only last month, a work colleague had been rushed to hospital after suffering a stroke.

Sometimes Laurie wanted to get hit by a bus and die just so she could come back as a ghost and tell Jeremy, 'I told you we shouldn't have waited!'

But it was more than the drudgery of work and the fear of declining health. If she was absolutely honest, Laurie was pretty much fed up with everything. She often felt like she was the only one seeing all the bad behaviour in the world. Not just all the big stuff like countries invading one another, but all the little bits of bad behaviour too like people just knocking into you as they got off the train, people swinging their bags right into your legs, or the countless ways Jeremy seemed to like to make her life so much trickier than it needed to be by leaving drawers open, chairs not tucked under tables, shoes strewn all over the hallway, loo rolls left unreplaced. Sometimes, she just wanted to stand in the middle of the kitchen or the train station and howl, 'Am I the only person that's seeing all this?' She truly felt that she was.

Did anybody else feel the way she did? Did her work colleagues have the same restlessness? Maybe it was the menopause – maybe her hormones were causing chaos and she'd calm down at some point. Was menopause a second adolescence? A sort of female reset button? Whatever it was, Laurie felt that it was time to change things up a bit.

It was then that she remembered Sally in Accounts. She was always threatening to leave the company and go travelling. Perhaps she was feeling the same restlessness that Laurie was.

After sorting out the muddle with the double-booked meeting room, Laurie left her desk and went to find Sally. When she entered her friend's office, Sally was glaring at her computer. She didn't look like she was in a good mood.

'Sal?'

'Laurie!' She looked up from her laptop, her eyes red-rimmed.

'Ready for a tea break?'

'Ready for a gin break. A *double* one!'

'Oh, dear!' Laurie said. 'Well, I might have a cure for you.'

'Really?'

'Now, don't go getting excited. It's not alcohol. But I think it might actually be better.'

'Better than alcohol?'

Laurie grinned and nodded.

Ten minutes later and onto their second cup of tea, Laurie had put forward her idea of them going away together.

'Where were you thinking of?' Sally asked.

'*Anywhere!*' Laurie said excitedly. 'Well, Europe. Let's not go totally crazy. I'm not sure I've got the budget for crazy.'

'Somewhere warm,' Sally suggested.

'Definitely! With mountains.'

'And the sea,' Sally added.

Laurie nodded. They were definitely on the same page. 'I've always wanted to see dolphins in the wild.'

'Yes!'

'So somewhere like Italy or the Canary Islands?'

Sally was beaming as she nodded. 'Oh, Laurie! Can we really make this happen?'

'If we put our minds to it – yes!'

'I'll have to check with Phil,' Sally said, suddenly looking anxious.

Laurie hadn't even considered what Jeremy might say, but she'd already decided that she was not going to wait a moment longer and, if Jeremy didn't want to go, he couldn't blame her if she went with somebody else, could he?

'I'm so fed up of our weather,' Sally went on. 'I want to

wear a dress again. Imagine that – just a dress! No sweater, no coat. Maybe even no bra or knickers! Just a light cotton dress to waft around in.'

Laurie giggled. 'And I want to explore – to see something more than offices and kitchens, and this – this town!'

Sally nodded. 'What made you think of asking me?'

'Well, you're always talking about wanting to travel. And...' she paused.

'What?'

'I'm a bit too nervous to do it on my own.'

Sally gave her a warm smile. 'I think that's what's been holding me back too.'

'So Phil doesn't want to go with you?'

'Nah! He's wedded to Cornwall and Devon. I seriously can't get him to go anywhere else.'

Laurie wrinkled her nose at that.

'Don't get me wrong – they're beautiful! But I feel like I've wrung all the secrets out of them. You know what I mean? If I have to see one more fishing village or tin mine, I swear I'll go mad!'

Laurie laughed. 'Listen, we'd better get back to work.'

'I'll text you tonight, okay? Once I've spoken with Phil.'

Laurie could barely concentrate on work after that. She was just too excited. This was going to happen. They were going to *make* it happen. She was only annoyed with herself that she hadn't suggested it to Sally sooner. But there was no point in having regrets. You could only ever start from where you were and Laurie was going to make the most brilliant start ever. With Sally!

That night, Laurie waited anxiously for Sally to message her. She'd put off telling Jeremy her plans until Sally had confirmed she could go, but Laurie couldn't resist taking a tentative look at flights and hotels in the Canary Islands. It seemed like the best bet for all year round sunshine and was just a four hour flight away. Oh, to feel warm again, she thought wistfully. Properly warm. What was it Sally had said? To waft around in a cotton dress? Laurie could picture them – two rebels living their best lives in the sunshine.

Maybe this was just the beginning too. Maybe this could be an annual thing.

Laurie shook her head. Why wait a whole year between trips? Maybe they could do two or even three? Or...

She paused, trying desperately not to get carried away only finding it was impossible. Maybe they could take a sabbatical – a grown-up gap year and really see something of the world. Laurie's mind raced at the idea. They'd need backpacks, train passes, guidebooks.

'Vaccinations!' Laurie blurted as she loaded the dishwasher later that night.

'What was that?' Jeremy looked up from his newspaper at the kitchen table.

'Nothing. Just thinking of something.'

He frowned and returned to the sports page.

Laurie quickly left the room to check her phone again. There was a message from Sally. At last! Laurie opened it and gasped. But not with joy.

I'm sorry. I don't think I'll be able to go.

Laurie closed her eyes, allowing herself a dark moment of disappointment. And then she read the rest of her friend's message.

It turned out that Phil had been super supportive of the idea but then Sally had started to have misgivings. About safety, about money and about going without Phil – even though he didn't want to go.

That night, Laurie switched her phone off, not trusting herself to reply tonight for fear of upsetting Sally as she was feeling so let down. But Sally genuinely sounded sorry and she genuinely sounded scared. Even the fact that she'd be going with Laurie couldn't allay her fears. She'd made up her mind and the answer was no.

In a desperate moment, not wanting to let the dream evaporate completely, Laurie switched her phone back on and messaged Tilly.

Want a free holiday to the Canary Islands?

She didn't have to wait long for an answer.

Awwww, Mum! Sweet of you, but I can't spare the time away from work at the mo. xxx

Of course she couldn't. Laurie couldn't expect her busy daughter to just drop everything.

She walked through to the en suite of her and Jeremy's bedroom and sat on the edge of the bath, deliberating for a moment, and then texted her son.

Fancy a free holiday to Tenerife with your old mum? X

The reply that came back wasn't as quick nor was it as kind as his sister's. It was a row of emojis – most of them laughing faces. Laurie shouldn't have messaged him. And she certainly shouldn't have emphasised the word "old", but perhaps she'd been playing the sympathy card. Well, that hadn't worked, had it? And to think of all the cold football matches she'd endured over the years. Not that she begrudged him. She'd done it willingly and lovingly. But she just kind of wished it all counted for a little bit more reciprocity when she needed it most.

She switched her phone off again, went downstairs and back into the kitchen. Jeremy was still at the table with his newspaper, settled for the evening. With any luck, he wouldn't notice her.

'Laurie?' She heard the rattle of his paper as he put it down.

Damn it, she thought, her hand in mid-air as she reached into the cupboard where the jammy dodgers were hiding.

'Yes?' she said innocently.

'You told me to stop you from late night snacking, didn't you?'

'Not in times of crisis.'

'What crisis?'

She closed the cupboard door and turned to face him. If he wasn't going to let her have a jammy dodger, he could jolly well go to Tenerife with her.

'I want us to go away, Jeremy. Somewhere warm. Somewhere exciting!'

'Oh, not this again.' He picked up his newspaper. 'You know my feelings. I don't like airports or flying. It's a huge waste of time and money.'

Laurie immediately translated that as him telling her that *she* was a waste of time and money.

'But *I* want to go,' she said, hating how childish she sounded now.

'Law – let me read my paper, okay? It's been a long day.'

It's been a long year, Laurie couldn't help thinking, reaching back into the cupboard before cramming a rebellious jammy dodger into her mouth in front of him.

She returned upstairs to run a bath. A nice deep, warm bath always made her feel better.

As she slipped into the water, submerging her shoulders in the scented bubbles, she tried to think who else she could ask.

Nobody.

Nobody wanted to go with her. No – that wasn't strictly true, perhaps. Tilly might have gone if she wasn't so busy. And Sally had so clearly wanted to go, but she was letting her fears get the better of her.

As Laurie soaked, slowly letting the water cool around her, something became absolutely clear and she didn't know why she hadn't considered it before. She just couldn't shake the images of the Canary Islands she'd seen when searching online. She *knew* she had to get there. And she also knew that, if she was going to do this, she'd have to do it alone.

CHAPTER SIX

The relief was like nothing Elise has ever known. No more visits to the stuffy, lightless living room. No more confrontations and barked orders from The Chair.

No more Mother.

Of course, the relief flooded in with a good old dose of guilt. After all, her mother's condition had not been her choice. But surely there were people with health issues who still managed to be kind and who didn't attack those around them with vitriolic words and mean glances. Still, the suddenness of her death had been shocking although Elise felt as if she'd been mourning her mother all her life because of their distinctly odd relationship. Marie had never *felt* like a mother. There'd been no warmth, no compassion. Elise hadn't known that wasn't normal until she'd visited a friend's house when she'd been about seven and met *her* mother.

Mrs Richards had been so kind and it wasn't a one-off kindness shown when a friend visits just the once and a show is put on. Elise had visited her friend's house many times over the years and she'd seen the genuine warmth between her friend Belinda and her mother. They'd been so comfortable in each other's company. Belinda was never on edge as Elise often was. She wasn't wary of her mother's presence in a room the way Elise was, or anxious about what might come out of her mouth. And they talked too. They were able to chat and share moments together. And laugh. Imagine that! Elise had felt so jealous and almost resentful for a while because it had made her realise how unlucky she was.

So she'd been mourning her mother for many years really.

Her brother, Michael, had come over for the funeral, but Elise couldn't be totally sure that he would have made the time and stumped up the air fare if his favourite eighties band hadn't had been on a revival tour in the UK and were playing in their home town the very same week. It had been good to see him again after so many years. How many had it been? At least fifteen since he'd emigrated, Elise thought. He'd aged. His hair had receded and silvered and his face looked a little drawn behind the Australian tan. But, then again, she'd aged too, hadn't she? Elise still got a shock when she realised that she was fifty-four. Those years had crept up on her, leaving a wrinkle here and a grey hair there. She was lucky that she had good skin and not too many grey hairs despite her mother's draining energy over the years.

Michael had offered to stay to help sort the house out, but Elise could see his heart wasn't in it and he was itching to get back home. He'd done a token clear-up of general mess – he'd taken a few items to charity and helped bring boxes and suitcases down from the loft to make it easier for Elise to go through them. He'd also engaged the estate agent and solicitor to get things moving. And then he'd left.

'Keep in touch,' he'd said and Elise had wondered if she'd ever see him again. Would he even come over for her funeral? It seemed like such an enormous waste of time, energy and money to her and she wouldn't blame him if he didn't.

The funeral was months ago now and, mercifully, probate and the sale of the house had gone through quickly. However Elise still had a room full of her mother's possessions in her second bedroom. It had all seemed so overwhelming at the time and she'd taken some of the boxes and suitcases that seemed to be full of more personal things like photo albums to sort through another time.

So was now 'another time'? Her brother had told her not to get sentimental about a load of old stuff and to be shot of the lot, but Elise couldn't bear to do that. She needed to go through it piece by piece even if it was a kind of slow torture. She wasn't sure if she was looking for anything in particular – little glimpses of a time when they'd been happy, perhaps? A time when her mother hadn't snipped and sniped at her?

So, this rainy Sunday afternoon, she'd dragged one of the suitcases out and taken it downstairs into her living room where there was more light to look through the photo albums it contained. The first three enormous albums she flipped through contained photos in black and white. Sepia too. Time-worn, forgotten faces. There were no labels. No names or dates to help her identify who any of them might be. A few more recent albums contained colour photos and Elise saw images of relatives with the same features as her. Not her red hair, of course – that trait had been from her father's side and there weren't any photos of him or his relatives for some reason.

It was sad, she thought. Now her mother was gone, there

was nobody who knew who these people were. Who had they been and what kind of lives had they led? Had they been happy? Had they loved life? Did they have descendants somewhere who Elise didn't know about? And what was she to do with them all? She didn't feel it was right to just bin them although she knew that was exactly what somebody else would do after her death, so why should she have the angst of hanging on to them?

She packed them all away. She hadn't found the photo albums from her own childhood yet and wasn't really in the mood to look at them now. But, as she returned the suitcase to the bedroom, she saw another much smaller case which she'd shoved under the guest bed and couldn't resist pulling it out. It looked old. Pre-First World War at least. Brown and slightly tatty, but still strong.

'And heavy,' Elise said out loud as she bent her knees and picked it up and took it into the living room. She'd forgotten how heavy it had been when she'd brought it here and wondered what was inside it. She hadn't so much as peeked before. She'd been so tired shifting everything from her mother's place to hers. She'd just assumed it would be more photo albums.

But it wasn't. At least, not exactly. It was full of sketchbooks. Dozens of them. Each with a hard cover which had kept the pages clean and tight for so many years. Elise's breath caught as she saw a date in pencil in the bottom right-hand corner of a landscape in watercolour.

'1901.'

She looked at the landscape again. It didn't look English although the gentle hills were green. There was something Tuscan about it, Elise thought. She turned the page and smiled. Now there was a sight you couldn't mistake.

Brunelleschi's dome in Florence. Her fingers hovered over the image. Who had painted it so beautifully? And had whoever it was been to Florence in 1901? Or was it drawn from a photograph or perhaps even another painting?

Elise couldn't help noting that Florence in the early nineteen hundreds was when one of her favourite heroines Lucy Honeychurch had visited in E M Forster's classic novel *A Room with a View*. Oh, the countless times she had read that book and watched the glorious film adaptation. Many a winter's evening had been warmed by the Tuscan countryside as shot in the glorious Merchant Ivory film, and Elise had tried to imagine what it must be like to wander the streets around Santa Croce as those beloved characters had – and as she'd almost managed to do on the trip she'd been called home from.

She thought once again of the life that might have been. Clearly, she wasn't the only one in her family who hankered after Italy? It made her curious to know who they had been so she continued to bring out sketchbook after sketchbook. There were dozens of them – some much larger containing watercolours which could easily have been framed, and others like the kind you'd pop into a handbag and take out in the street to capture a detail. Elise particularly loved those ones. There were several of Italy with gorgeous architectural details such as gargoyles, arches, windows and doors – just the sort of things she always looked out for when she visited anywhere. Maybe she'd inherited her distant ancestor's sensibilities, she thought fancifully.

She continued looking through the albums. Most of them were of Italy, but there were a few from southern Spain – places she recognised and longed to see for herself like the Alhambra in Granada and the Mezquita in Cordoba. It seemed as if this ancestor had definitely favoured the warmer climes of southern Europe – another thing Elise felt she had in common with this person, even though she hadn't managed to get there herself yet other than that aborted trip to Florence.

It was as she turned one of the pages that she discovered a photograph. A lovely rounded-at-the-edges sepia-soft photograph of a woman.

'Found you!' she cried. If, indeed, it was the artist.

She was beautiful. Her hair was long and thick and was pinned around her head in a halo as was the fashion of the time. Her expression was serious and yet there was a softness about it. Elise suspected that she was posing for the camera and had been told to keep very still as they had to in those days, but she could easily imagine this beautiful face was capable of the warmest smiles. Her left hand looked slightly clenched betraying possible unease. Maybe she was more comfortable being the artist rather than the subject.

Her dress looked impossibly tight around her waist and had a high lacy neckline that Elise knew would make her itch if she had to wear it. Everything was lacy and frilly and the long sleeves of her dress puffed out like meringues and were trimmed with even more lace. How on earth had women moved about in those days – let alone travelled? Had she worn such an outfit while sketching in the streets of Italy or Spain?

Elise turned the photograph over and there in fine pencil was a name written in beautiful script.

Clara Beech.

Now her mystery ancestor had a face and a name!

Unfortunately, there was no date, but the clothes definitely suggested she was Edwardian. Elise had never heard the name before and yet she was clearly a relative unless someone in her family had brought the suitcase full of sketchbooks which didn't seem very likely. How frustrating that her mother had never mentioned her and that Elise couldn't ask about her now. But perhaps her mother wouldn't have known anything anyway. Maybe she had inherited the suitcase herself from her own mother. It was quite possible that she hadn't even looked inside it.

Elise decided that Clara Beech must be a great great aunt at least, and she was delighted to discover her name once again written in the back of the first Italian sketchbook when she looked a second time – clearly linking the woman with the sketches.

How extraordinary for her to have been to all these places especially back when travel wasn't quite as quick, easy or comfortable as it was today – especially for women on their own. But maybe she hadn't been on her own. Maybe she'd had a companion or even a family. There was no evidence either way and yet Elise couldn't help thinking that there surely would have been a sketch of a child or a husband or a friend had they been accompanying her.

Elise smiled. How easy it was to create a narrative. A few minutes ago, she hadn't known of this woman's existence and now the woman she had christened 'Great Aunt Clara' was an intrepid Edwardian spinster who'd travelled with nothing but her sketchbook and watercolours.

Elise thought about her own great wish to see more of the world as she looked at the sketches and paintings again. Especially the Italian ones. The country seemed to have been a great draw for Clara too – in all meanings of the word, she thought with a grin.

And then an idea occurred to her. With her recent

inheritance, she could go to Italy again. Her responsibility to her mother had always stopped her from taking time away from her home town. But now she was free of that responsibility and she couldn't help thinking that the inheritance meant she could take something of a sabbatical from her job. After all, she'd accrued quite a bit of leave from the years she'd hardly taken any time off work.

A sudden excitement filled her as she flipped through the pages of the sketchbooks again. There were so many places she could see at last. So much beauty. So many experiences she could gift herself. The options were limitless which was a little overwhelming and might just kill her dream before she let it blossom.

And then something occurred to her. Why not arrange a trip around the places her Great Aunt Clara had visited? Elise longed to see more of the world, but the thought of putting an itinerary together with such vague aspirations as 'see more of the world' was somewhat daunting. Other than Italy – and maybe Spain – she had no idea where to go.

She looked at the photo of Clara Beech again. Her expression was kind and gentle.

'You could be my guide,' Elise whispered and the tiniest of butterflies began to flutter deep inside her as a plan began to form.

CHAPTER SEVEN

It was the most wonderful feeling in the world, Nu thought as she hit the main road and dared to build up a bit of speed. After the initial panic of manocuvring the vehicle out of the driveway, across town and negotiating her first roundabout, she was feeling a little more confident. She might not have left the country yet, but she was giving herself the time she needed to get to know The Van and how to take care of everything that van life threw at her.

She was calling it her Training Time and she'd combined it with a trip she'd always wanted to do to Stonehenge and Glastonbury. Paul had always laughed at her when she'd said she wanted to see the famous stone circle and the old town, dismissing its history and mystery as "a load of hippie nonsense". But Nu had been thrilled by it all – the majesty of the huge grey stones rising up from the flat landscape of Salisbury Plain, and the little shops selling wonderfully crazy things that Paul would never have allowed her to buy. Just to spite him, she bought herself a clear quartz crystal on a blue ribbon to hang up in The Van. With any luck, it would negate any bad vibes he might be sending her.

She'd even driven up to Avebury and spent a very happy couple of hours photographing the stone circle there. It was lovely to simply lose herself in the moment and forget about the pain of the last few weeks. In fact, she was thinking of documenting her journey on YouTube. She didn't imagine that anyone would be interested, but it might be a fun project to undertake. Learn a new skill. Share her thoughts. Who knows – she might just inspire somebody else to take the plunge and hit the road on their own. She herself had been watching a lot of YouTube travellers. She'd found many inspirational men and women who had taken to the open road in their vehicles from old VW campervans and converted school buses to the most luxurious modern motorhomes on the market complete with all mod cons. Nu knew she was lucky with her brand-new vehicle with its tiny kitchen area, shower and toilet. It was, perhaps, a little too luxurious for her needs and she couldn't help feeling guilty about the space she had just for herself when she saw what others were driving around the world in. But she'd worked hard for this and she wasn't about to downsize her dream just because her husband had dumped her. She was determined to live her very best life.

Still, sleeping alone in the double bed felt a little odd especially when she remembered the night they'd given it a test drive, so to speak. She kind of wished they hadn't gone out in The Van together now. She'd just have to erase that particular memory because The Van was *hers*. This adventure was *hers*.

Leaving the county of Somerset behind, her mind trawled back over the last few weeks. The house sale had gone through smoothly and, of course, Paul had been trying to get hold of her. Where was she? And, more to the point – where was The Van? She'd deleted all his messages and had refused to answer his calls. She knew she'd have to talk to him eventually, but not yet. Let him sweat a bit first. Let *him* experience some pain and anxiety. Heaven knew he'd put her through enough of that recently.

The only thing she was concerned about – other than the whole managing absolutely everything on her own such as van maintenance and navigating her way around Europe – was the loneliness. She hated to admit it but she'd been surrounded by others all her life and was kind of used to it. Whether it had been her family, the busy office or her marriage, Nu had always had *someone*. And the truth was she wasn't sure how to operate in the world alone.

Perhaps that's why she'd turned to social media. She'd joined a few online groups for things like van living and driving across Europe, and she'd subscribed to many YouTube channels where intrepid women were living life to the full and documenting their journeys. She'd been watching one woman who'd just started a channel and was filming her journey from the north of Scotland down to southern Spain. And it was really inspiring Nu to get on with starting her own channel. She could do something similar – film her journey, capturing her thoughts, her fears and her adventures. It would be a wonderful way to not only document her journey but to connect with others. She was blown away by the information that people shared on YouTube. It was a constant source of inspiration and encouragement and Nu felt that it was something she could contribute to. It would certainly be a good way to fill in the lonely hours in the evenings and a fun way to capture her travels.

But it was one thing to dream about creating a YouTube channel and quite another thing to actually do it. Nuala had quickly realised the amount of work involved. She wasn't the most technically literate person in the world – that role in their marriage had been Paul's. He was the one to set up new computers, phones and any other electronic device and to sort them out whenever they misbehaved. But she'd managed to set up an account and had had a few goes filming herself. When she'd watched the footage back, she'd cringed. Did she really look like that? What was going on with her hair? Should she wear more make-up? Would she need to get her teeth whitened? Would anybody really want to watch a middle-aged woman driving a van all over Europe, moaning on about how her husband had left her?

And all those insecurities came before she'd actually attempted speaking to the camera. She'd quickly realised that the camera on her phone was good enough but that she'd need a tripod and microphone if she was to make a decent video. Lighting was important too but she'd decided she'd shoot outdoors when she could and use natural daylight. She wanted to keep things as real as possible, even if she had bought teeth-whitening toothpaste and a mascara which promised to lift and curl her meagre eyelashes.

But who was she kidding? She didn't have the courage for this. This was a young person's world, wasn't it? All those sassy young women who'd been brought up attached to a ring light and mobile phone. Those digital nomads who thought nothing about talking to the camera without a script – just spilling out whatever was in their heads. And yet there were plenty of older women doing this and their content had been inspiring Nu so much. Indeed, she'd even bought a special notebook in which she'd ambitiously started to jot down ideas for her channel.

She had to catch herself and laugh at the phrase 'her channel'. Who did she think she was? That's what the devil on her shoulder would taunt her with. But there was the angel on her other shoulder. 'You are Nuala Marshall – and you've survived a terrible betrayal and gone on to have a great adventure!'

At the moment, her channel had the rather dull name of "Nuala's New Life" and she knew she'd have to come up with something better. The name was too generic and could refer to anything from taking on a DIY project to opening a beach café in Bali. She chewed the end of her pen as her mind whirled with possibilities. It was important to make a good first impression and to capture viewers' attention.

"Nuala's Road Trip" might work, but it was a bit dull. What about "Nuala's European Adventure"? She wrote it down and looked at it. Would that give the wrong impression? Would people expect more than a woman in her fifties driving?

And then another idea popped into her head.

"Nuala and The Van"

She paused. She liked that one. It was simple and it said everything. And she could add a little tagline to her YouTube banner explaining more. She grinned. This was exciting. She could practically feel her synapses snapping.

She made a list of words she liked and that she felt encapsulated where she was in her life.

Retired. New adventures. Road trip. Freedom. Fifties. Single.

Her breath caught as she read the last one again. Single.

That had never been in her grand plan, had it? And yet here she was. Maybe she should be honest about that on her channel. Maybe she could inspire other women who were going through something similar.

She thought of some other words – some *honest* words.

Excited. Hopeful. Determined. Frightened.

Again, it was the last word that caught her off-guard. So, here she was: single and frightened.

She shook her head. She wanted to be honest, but she didn't want to depress people. And yet she instinctively knew you could be both single and frightened and still inspire others – if you spoke from a place of truth and kindness and if you were willing to put yourself out there even when absolutely everything terrified you.

Nuala and The Van...

Figuring Life out One Road at a Time.

She stared at the words she'd written. The tagline showed both her trepidation and optimism. She was doing her best – figuring things out *as she went*. She didn't really have a plan for any of this. Her plan had gone out of the window when Paul had announced he was leaving her. The 'one road at a time' was both literal and metaphorical.

But what would everyone think of this new venture into YouTube? What would her ex-work colleagues think? What would her family think?

'What will Paul think?' she asked out loud.

She decided not to tell anyone. The general advice she'd heard about starting a YouTube channel was that you shouldn't tell your friends and family because most of them really wouldn't care and it was important – especially in the embryonic stages of creation – that nobody killed your dream. Besides, she rather liked having this new, secret life. It was a private incarnation that nobody needed to know about. It was for her alone. Well, her and any viewers who happened to discover her online – the fellow souls who needed to hear her message just as much as she needed to share it.

So, over the next few weeks, as she slowly adjusted to van life – navigating country lanes in a large vehicle, finding suitable places to stop, and emptying the dreaded toilet cassette, Nu also learned how to speak to the camera and how to upload her recordings and edit them down into something that approached a watchable video. She was going to keep things simple. No fancy edits. No special effects. No music drowning things out. Just her and her musings on her newly single life as she drove around Europe.

The first time she uploaded one was the most nerve-wracking experience of her life. Her fingers hovered over the publish button for what seemed like an eternity.

You can always delete it, the devil's voice told her. *Nobody will see it anyway.*

Everything will be fine, the angel's voice told her. *Others need to hear your story!*

But what if they didn't like it? What if they left hateful messages? What if they criticised the way she looked? Or the way she drove? Or what she had to say?

Nuala spent a long time thinking all this over. It was one of the risks you took when stepping out of your comfort zone. If you wanted to connect with the world, you couldn't stay hidden away from it. So she uploaded her first video and waited. It was a simple one – a tour of The Van and a few shots of her driving through the English countryside, touching lightly on how she had unexpectedly found herself alone on the road. She wasn't sure what to expect from launching and she spent an inordinate amount of time checking her viewing figures. She tried not to but it was addictive. Addictive and unhealthy.

She tried to ration herself.

I won't look until I've gone shopping and done the dishes.

I'll only look first thing in the morning and last thing at night.

I won't look until I've driven fifty miles.

Then, when she could stand it no longer, she looked. Twenty-four views. It wasn't ground-breaking or earth-shattering, but it was a start. A definite start. A few kind souls had even hit the "like" button below the video.

But, when she awoke the next morning, she gasped. Not only had her viewer count gone up to seventy-one, but there was a comment from someone called RozinRome.

Good for you, Honey! Keep driving and thriving!

Nu's heart swelled with the praise.

'I can do this,' she said. And then she corrected herself and spoke with a little more conviction.

'I *am* doing this!'

CHAPTER EIGHT

How often did you get to claim your own headspace these days, Laurie wondered? If it wasn't being filled by the draining daily tasks you had to do at home and at work, it was snatched away by advertisers coming at you from whatever social media platform you happened to be browsing. Waking hours were filled by an endless stream of demands and tasks and then, when you tried to escape for five minutes of innocent scrolling on your phone, companies were trying to sell you something and take that little bit of hard-earned money you'd done your best to squirrel away for a rainy day.

And don't get her started on the many people who were offering 'free' courses online. Just sign up here for your free seminar/conference/workshop. Whatever they called it, it was all about the upsell once you'd been sucked in. The freebie was just a taster, but what you really needed was whatever they were selling. Of course, that was at a knockdown price for this week only. It was only £297 or £497 or £897. Any price really as long as it ended in a seven.

But it was actually worth *at least* three times that price. So don't miss out because you'll only have this opportunity now.

Sometimes Laurie's head hurt with the weight of information that was coming her way and she longed to get away from it all.

She was feeling particularly low after Sally had backed out of their great plan to break free together. And her friend obviously felt awkward about the situation because she'd definitely been trying to avoid Laurie at work. So now Laurie felt as if she'd lost a friend on top of everything else.

She'd been having a tough week at home too. Sometimes, she felt like she was just a member of staff as far as her family was concerned – there to provide a service like fresh laundry, a cooked dinner, a free taxi service. So often they would speak *at* her rather than *to* her and they certainly didn't listen if she ever tried to talk to them. Not really. They were just thinking of what they would say next.

It felt so very lonely.

Maybe *all* these things had played their part in driving her towards her decision to leave. At first, Laurie had thought a holiday might be enough to sate her but, the more she thought about it, the more she realised that she needed a complete change. Each little hurt she'd endured might not have been enough on its own, but so many together had an avalanche-like momentum and she knew things had to change for good. But there was still so much to sort out, although she had at least told her boss at work and had been able to negotiate taking voluntary redundancy. The look on her face had been priceless. Amanda Farthing had just assumed that somebody like Laurie would be chained to her desk until every little bit of her had been drained by the company. Then and only then would she limp into retirement.

Laurie had glanced around Amanda's office and spotted a couple of industry awards. She had a career to be proud of, but at what price had it come, Laurie couldn't help thinking? There was a pile of papers on her desk and heaven only knew how many emails in her inbox. All that time allocated. Time she wouldn't be spending with loved ones or under the blue canopy of the sky, or walking through a shady forest or up a mountain with the wind in her hair and the sun on her cheeks. But maybe she didn't want to climb a mountain and maybe she preferred time in an office to time spent out in the world. Who knew? You couldn't choose somebody else's life for them. That was something Laurie was learning fast these days. Everyone had a right to pursue what made them happy, and what lit one person up might leave another feeling thoroughly drained.

It all came to a head at the weekend after Laurie had spoken to Amanda Farthing. Tilly and Joseph had come over for Sunday lunch and were arguing in the kitchen as Laurie was trying to prepare everything.

'He won't listen, Mum!' Tilly was complaining. 'He's just like Dad!'

'What?' Jeremy barked from over the Sunday paper – a huge doorstep of a publication which would take him all day to get through which meant he wasn't going to help with getting lunch organised.

'Yeah, well you're so perfect, aren't you?' Joseph cried. 'Always sucking up to Mum so you can borrow more money.'

'I do not!' Tilly complained.

'No?'

Laurie glanced at her daughter and saw that her cheeks were flaming. Only last week, she'd *borrowed* another thirty pounds from Laurie.

The meal, once on the table, was eaten in a sulky silence that made Laurie feel both resentful and sad. Who were these people she was sitting with? She truly didn't recognise them anymore. She certainly didn't recognise herself. When had the change occurred? Was it purely menopausal? Was she going through the dreaded midlife crisis? Or was she having some sort of spiritual awakening and so was suddenly able to cut through all the nonsense and see it for what it was?

Laurie sat there, watching as her son pushed his Yorkshire pudding into a pool of gravy while his sister ate without using her knife because her right thumb was used for scrolling her phone. Laurie had long given up trying to enforce the 'no phone' rule at the table during meals. Nobody listened to her.

'Nobody's listening to me!'

'Mum?' Tilly glanced up from her phone.

Laurie gasped. Had she said that out loud?

Even Joseph and Jeremy were looking at her now.

'I said...' she paused. 'Nobody's eating the peas.' She pushed the extra bowl of peas she'd prepared to the centre of the table. For years, it had been the only greens she could get Joseph to eat.

'I've gone off them,' Joseph told her.

'I've had enough,' Tilly said.

Laurie took them after Jeremy shook his head. She'd be eating them for the next three days now. Another role she'd fallen into over the years: human dustbin – eating all the leftovers to save wasting food.

It was something of a surprise when Tilly offered to help tidy the kitchen and wash the pans after lunch. However, it wasn't such a surprise when she sidled up to her by the sink, a guilty expression on her face. Laurie knew what was coming.

'Mum?' Tilly began, stretching the word out so that it sounded as if it had three syllables. 'I hate to ask again. I know I owe you absolutely *loads* by now – and I promise to pay it all back. I'm bound to get that promotion at work and it'll all be fine after that.'

'What do you need?' Laurie asked matter-of-factly.

Tilly puffed her cheeks out. 'Fifty should cover it. Although eighty would be better.'

'Eighty?'

'Yes, tickets are rip-off prices these days.'

'What's it for?'

'That concert I told you about. Everyone's going! I can't miss it.'

Laurie thought back over the years and the many things she'd missed to raise her two children not only because of the cost but the time too. Neither had been her own to spend. But they were now.

'Tilly – I can't give you eighty pounds for a pop concert.'

'It's not pop,' Tilly protested. 'It's—'

'Well, I'm not sure that matters. What does matter is that you're not in a position to fund it yourself yet. A concert is a luxury, Tilly. You have to learn to do without such things when you're starting out or...' Laurie paused. Did she dare to say it? 'Or when you're raising a family. Just as your father and I did – for many, many years.'

'Oh, I see,' Tilly said, sounding resentful.

'No, darling. I don't think you do.' Laurie smiled at her

kindly. 'You mean the world to me and I hate to deny you anything, and I hope I haven't over the years. But I have denied myself, you see. For so many years and – well – I'm a bit fed up with that now.'

'Mum!' Tilly sounded shocked.

'You can ask your dad for the money if you want,' she told her daughter, knowing that she wouldn't dare. He wasn't such a soft touch.

Tilly shook her head and Laurie wondered if it was because she wasn't going to approach her father or if she was in disbelief that her mother had denied her something.

It wasn't just Tilly, mind. Laurie sometimes felt as if the whole world thought she was a soft touch. She'd heard a lot of noise online about 'victim mentality' recently. Was there such a thing as 'doormat mentality', Laurie wondered. She was beginning to think that there might be because the compounded years of her being treated like this by her family had made her act in a certain way around them. Well, she wasn't going to have it anymore.

For a moment, she looked around the kitchen. Jeremy had stacked some of the plates and cutlery in the dishwasher – badly – and was sitting back at the table with his enormous newspaper. Joseph was helping himself to her stash of jammy dodgers and Tilly was leaning against the Aga, biting her thumbnail and looking decidedly sulky after her request for money had been denied.

It was time.

She cleared her throat, suddenly feeling nervous.

'I've made a decision,' she announced.

'Can I have custard with mine?' Joseph said.

'What?' Laurie asked, confused.

'Dessert. That *is* what you're talking about, isn't it? That apple pie I saw in the fridge.'

'No, that isn't what I'm talking about. And that pie remains in the fridge. I'm going to eat it cold tonight when you two have gone and your father's snoring in bed.'

That got everybody's attention.

'What's going on?' Jeremy asked, finally putting his newspaper down and paying her attention.

'I'm going away,' Laurie told them. 'I've taken voluntary redundancy and I've worked out my period of notice.'

'What?' Jeremy said, somewhat perplexed by this news.

'I'm not waiting any more, Jeremy.'

Tilly glanced at Joseph who just shrugged.

'Your mother's having one of her moments,' Jeremy told them with a little chuckle, obviously choosing not to believe her.

'Oh, not the dreaded menopause!' Joseph said with an uncomfortable laugh. 'Everyone seems to be talking about that at the moment. You can't move on social media without a red-faced woman shouting at you!'

Jeremy barked out a laugh which made Laurie's insides heat up with rage and it wasn't a hot flush.

Only Tilly seemed to realise that she was deadly serious.

'Where are you going, Mum?'

Laurie cleared her throat. 'Spain. To begin with. A yoga retreat in Tenerife. And I've always wanted to see southern Spain. That Golden Triangle from Seville to Cordoba and Granada. Then down to the coast to Tarifa. Did you know you can get a boat to Africa from there? Imagine that – crossing continents by boat!'

Laurie gave a nervous sort of laugh. She'd been doing her

homework – plotting in secret – and yet it seemed so strange to be telling her family all this. 'And once I'm in Africa – who knows? Morocco, Tunisia, Egypt? I really don't know. But I do want to see the Canary Islands. All of them.' She paused. 'There are eight.'

Her heart was hammering so hard that she felt sure her family would be able to hear it above the whir of the dishwasher.

'Are you serious?' Joseph asked. He seemed to be paying her proper attention now. Perhaps regarding her as a real human being for the first time in his life – with needs and desires of her own.

She nodded. 'I've renewed my passport and I'm getting all my vaccinations, and I'll keep you all informed of where I am. Maybe we can set up a WhatsApp group or something. Anyway, that's my plan.'

'You won't do it,' Jeremy said, returning to his newspaper.

Joseph turned to look at his father and then back at his mother. 'I think she will.'

'I think she will too,' Tilly said. 'And you should.'

Laurie gasped, surprised to have the belief of her children.

'One of my friend's mums has just taken off to Thailand with a backpack,' Tilly said. 'She's doing the gap year she never did as a teenager.'

'That's a thing now, isn't it?' Joseph said. 'The grown-up gap year.'

Laurie nodded. 'Red-faced menopausal women rediscovering themselves.'

Joseph suddenly looked guilty. 'Sorry about that, Mum.'

'It's okay, darling.'

'When are you going?' Tilly asked.

'Next week if I can get myself organised.'

'What do you need to do?'

'Work out what I need to take with me. I'm trying to travel light, but clothes are my weakness.'

'Maybe I can help you.'

'Really?' Laurie was dumbfounded.

'Sure. It'll be fun!'

Laurie glanced at Jeremy whose nose was still deep in the literary supplement. He was the only one refusing to take part in this conversation.

'I'll help you set up your phone, Mum,' Joseph said. 'There are some awesome travel apps you should have.'

Laurie could feel tears threatening at the unexpected kindness of her children.

'Thank you,' she managed.

Joseph shrugged and Laurie could sense so much in that seemingly casual movement – it was his way of apologising, of showing he loved her and of wishing her well on her journey.

She'd been having so many doubts recently as to whether she'd been a good mother over the years and whether her children even liked her let alone loved her. But here they were ready to support her in her crazy new venture. She felt so very lucky.

Laurie was a little surprised when, just a week later, Jeremy drove her to the airport. If she was honest, she'd been a little reluctant for him to take her, saying she'd get a taxi, but he'd baulked at the cost. She'd rather have made a clean break than suffering his last-minute protestations. She did her best to zone him out, but negative words filled the car.

Irresponsible. Selfish. Unsafe.

She really should have got a taxi.

'I don't even know where you're going,' he said as they pulled into the mid stay car park.

'Yes you do. I've told you a dozen times and I've emailed you all the details.'

He shook his head.

'It's a yoga retreat in Tenerife.'

He swore under his breath.

'It's a group of twelve from all over the world. I've always wanted to do something like that.'

'But you can do yoga at home.'

'I do and it's not the same.'

'Or at the village hall if you must do it in public.'

She sighed. There was no point talking to him about any of this. He wouldn't understand in a million years.

'When will you be back?' he asked, sounding a little gentler now.

'I don't know.'

'What do you mean?'

'I've not decided. I want...' she paused, 'time.'

'For what?' His anger had returned again.

'For *me*, Jeremy! I need to think. Or *not* think. I don't know. I just need... time, okay?'

He nodded. Did he really understand this? She wasn't convinced.

They parked at the mid stay car park and got out of the car. Laurie grabbed her handbag. It was a new over the shoulder one with pockets galore. The strap was even reinforced which would prevent a thief from slicing through it. She was also wearing a neat money belt under her jumper. She wasn't taking any chances travelling alone.

She watched as Jeremy popped the boot open and lifted her backpack out. She'd bought herself a modest-sized one because she'd only ever had huge suitcases in the past and was determined to travel light now. Trips in the UK in the car had always given her the luxury and laziness of packing way too much. But, when you were on your own and had to carry everything yourself, it made you reassess everything. And she'd read that it was no fun lugging a case – even a small one – up and down the steps and stairs of Europe and over the echoing cobbles of old towns.

'Do you want me to wait with you for the bus to the terminal?' he asked as he handed the backpack to her.

She could think of nothing worse. 'No. It's okay. You get back.'

He nodded. 'Right...'

She waited for him to finish his sentence with – well, she wasn't sure what with. A good luck wish, a last-minute checklist, a word of warning or – did she dare hope for a moment of intimacy?

'The bus,' he said a moment later, nodding towards where it was now pulling up.

'Right.'

And, before she could say anything more, Jeremy had hopped back into the car. Laurie grabbed her backpack and marched to the bus stop. There were a few people waiting there already. There was a woman with a backpack similar to her own and others with the sort of enormous suitcase that you could empty an entire wardrobe into. Laurie allowed herself a satisfied smile that she'd managed to get everything she needed into her backpack.

When the bus dropped her off at Departures a few minutes later and Laurie made her way towards security, she felt a sort of nervous excitement coursing through her entire body. She was truly on her own now.

The sense of freedom was quite overwhelming.

CHAPTER NINE

It was going to take some time to find herself, Elise knew that. For so many years, she'd lived in the shadow of her mother. It had been her mother's voice filling her head and her mother's demands coveting all her free time. That weight – that negativity – had been all-pervading, and there'd been little room for Elise in her own life.

When Elise looked in the mirror, it was hard to see herself. But there was one thing she was eternally thankful for – she didn't look like her mother. It had been one of the things her mother had despised her for.

'You're *so* like your father,' she'd say through gritted teeth.

Elise had heard the refrain so many times. Her hair. Her eyes. Her nose. Even her ears.

She examined her ears now. They were just ears. There was nothing extraordinarily offensive about them and yet her mother had had such an issue with them.

But she didn't want to carry the weight of the past with her any longer – at least not the past she had known. But the past belonging to the woman she had come to think of as her great aunt – well, that was another matter entirely. That past intrigued her. She could see why people became obsessed with family trees and tracking down relatives. It was all so exciting to discover a name – a link with your genetic ancestors – and to feel that connection while maintaining a safe distance just in case the person you were tracing had actually been an idiot in life.

Mind you, there was a part of Elise that wondered if her great aunt might have been just as awful as her mother. Was there any way of telling that from a photograph and a handful of sketchbooks? If there was nobody alive who remembered you and no written evidence, a whole personality could be erased and it would be as if they'd never existed at all. And yet Elise felt like she knew a little about this person from the gentle expression on her face in the photo that seemed to speak of kindness and understanding. The sketchbooks, too, showed a person clearly in touch with the beauty of the world around them. Clara Beech had the kind of sensibilities that responded to the shape made by a Gothic spire shooting into a sunset and a sense of humour that appreciated the funny expression on a gargoyle's face. Elise instinctively liked Clara and deemed her the perfect travel companion.

One of the hardest things Elise had to come to terms with was the money she'd inherited. She'd never really given much thought to what would be coming her way one day. She'd even been a little surprised that her mother had left her anything at all. Elise wouldn't have been at all shocked if her mother had left her entire estate to the local cats' home just to spite her daughter. But the will had been a simple affair, splitting everything equally between her and her brother and, once the house had been sold, there was quite a tidy sum.

And oh the guilt! To be able to pay her mortgage off and to have a bank account that looked so rosy after years of scrimping and saving and still feeling as if life had got the better of her. Not that Elise had ever gone without a meal. It was just that the daily strain of modern life took its toll. The endless cycle of working to pay bills in order to remain in exactly the same place – it all seemed so futile.

But did she deserve this windfall? Her brother had taken it in his stride, but Elise had experienced so many emotions about it.

'El – who does the money belong to if not us?' her brother had said when they'd talked about it via WhatsApp after the house sale had finally gone through. 'Just enjoy it! Live a little!'

Live a little. Elise had liked that and she'd been determined to do it too. The inheritance gave her permission to take time out from her job without any sort of guilt. It wasn't a fortune but, if she was careful, she could live a life on her own terms. It wasn't enough to live extravagantly. She wouldn't be staying in five-star hotels, or taking cruise ships around the world for months at a time – she wouldn't have wanted to do that anyway – but it was enough to allow her some time and space to explore the world a little. She saw it as a belated wage for the hours her mother had swallowed whole and the misery that had been doled out daily. And there was a part of her that saw it in lieu of the price of therapy she felt sure she could benefit from. But she wasn't going to hand a single penny over to a counsellor. She was going to keep it all. Travel would be her therapy.

Elise had been shackled to the Midlands town for so long

that she truly felt like her toes might have actually grown roots. The thought of being able to leave it at last was both crippling and liberating. Could she exist outside this place? Did she have what it took to make it in the outside world? Or would the fear of what might happen if she stepped out of her comfort zone keep her there forever? There was only one way to find out.

She had arranged everything with her boss who'd been very understanding even though Elise hadn't been able to tell her when she'd be back.

'I want to keep things... loose,' she'd said. It had sounded crazy even to her own ears, but at least it was honest. She didn't want to make any promises and she didn't want to be harnessed by any sort of boundaries or limitations because those had ruled her life up until this point.

She knew where she was going of course: Italy. She didn't care which part because she wanted to see it all – every city, every region, every bit of coastline – craggy, volcanic and sandy. Okay, so that might be a bit ambitious for one trip. She just knew that she had to get herself there and that it didn't really matter where she started.

Still, seeing as she had to choose, she would start with Florence. Firenze. The centre of the Renaissance. She'd always loved the word *renaissance*. There was something so magical about what it represented. A rebirth, a renewal, a reawakening. Like spring after winter or feasting after fasting. Maybe her trip would be a chance for her to have a renaissance of her own. Ever since the doomed trip she'd had to celebrate her thirtieth birthday, she'd longed to return to the place she hadn't had time to explore properly because of the stunt her mother had pulled. But her mother wasn't around to do that to her now. This time, Elise was free.

Packing was problematic. Elise just hadn't taken holidays like most people. She'd bought herself a suitcase – a nice small one which meant she didn't have to check in luggage. Not because she wanted to travel light but because she didn't like the thought of all her possessions leaving her sight. She wasn't taking any chances when it came to Great Aunt Clara's sketchbooks.

She was taking the three sketchbooks of Italy which meant that she couldn't take quite as many clothes as she wanted to. Still she reasoned that they sold clothes in Italy and she could always buy an extra bag once she was there. The other must-have item was her slightly battered paperback of E M Forster's *A Room with a View*. She tucked it into her handbag to reread at the airport and on the short flight, knowing that she wouldn't feel so alone with the Honeychurches, the Emersons, Miss Bartlett and Miss Lavish to accompany her.

What was it about Italy that stirred so many English souls, she wondered? England had beautiful architecture, didn't it? And a wonderful, varied coastline. Okay, so the cuisine didn't tickle the taste buds in quite the same way. A bag of greasy chips could never hope to compete with a plate of fresh pasta or an oven-fired pizza. But there was something else about Italy – other than the sun, of course. It had a special kind of romanticism that stirred the soul and kept tourists flooding its iconic shores year after year.

Like with her first trip, Elise had booked herself a little apartment a five-minute stroll away from the River Arno on the Oltrano side of Florence. It was an arty district and prices there weren't quite as extortionate as the centre of the city which meant that she could spend longer on her dream trip. She might have inherited a healthy sum of money, but it wasn't a bottomless pit and she could easily burn through it if she lived extravagantly. And Elise wanted to linger for as long as possible.

~

The air was apple crisp that first morning in Florence, reminding Elise that it was still a long way off summer. She crossed the Ponte Vecchio – the famous old bridge which had, mercifully, escaped being bombed during the Second World War. The shops selling gold jewellery were all shuttered up. It was too early for tourists and Elise wallowed romantically in having the place virtually to herself. She'd waited a long time for this moment – The Me Moment, she thought with a smile. Me at last. She paused in the middle of the bridge to look down into the water and out towards the Palazzo Vecchio and the spot where Julian Sands and Helena Bonham Carter had stood in the film adaptation of *A Room with a View*. She, too, would stand there later. She would find all the locations used in both the book and the film as well as those in Great Aunt Clara's sketchbook. She had all the time in the world to do exactly what pleased her.

She was walking beside the River Arno when her phone rang. It was such a shrill and unexpected sound that she berated herself for having switched it on, but she'd wanted to use the camera. Who on earth could be ringing her so early? It was probably some scam call.

When she checked the screen, she didn't recognise the number. Definitely a scam. She debated answering it at all.

'Hello?' she said a moment later.

'Miss Cherrington? It's Doctor Reese. I'm afraid there's been a terrible mistake. Your mother's alive, but she's very distressed because everyone told her she was dead. I know you're abroad at the moment, but is there any way you can get back? We really need you here *right* away.'

Elise felt her chest tighten. The Florentine world tilted alarmingly and she felt the ground rise up to meet her. As she hit it, hard, her eyes snapped open and she gasped for breath.

She was in bed, her face hot and wet with tears.

She took a moment to remember where she was – or rather *when* she was.

You're okay, she told herself. *She's dead. She can't call you home because she's not there. She's gone and you're here.*

She swung her legs out of bed and crossed to the tiny fridge in the apartment and reached inside for a bottle of water, gulping it down before reaching for the second one and holding it to her face to cool down.

Logic might tell her that her mother was dead, but her subconscious obviously still needed convincing. It was going to take more than death and a funeral to banish her mother from her psyche.

She walked to the window and drew the curtains. Her apartment looked out onto a sweet courtyard surrounded by residential buildings. She let her eyes focus on it for a moment as she took some deep, stilling breaths. The nightmare had felt so real. The *feeling* of it. Her emotions. A part of her wanted to ring her brother. He was the only one who would understand, but she didn't want to trouble him. He'd probably moved on from their mother's death weeks ago, resigning it firmly to the past where it belonged. But how long would it take Elise to do that?

She was so annoyed with herself that, along with her dreams and her great aunt's sketchbooks, she'd somehow managed to pack all her old insecurities for this trip.

She tried to sluice all the drama of her nightmare away in the shower and, after a quick breakfast, she left the apartment for her first morning exploring. By the time she reached the Ponte Vecchio for real, the shutters of the jewellery shops had been opened and tourists had flooded the space. Elise didn't mind. She quite enjoyed the jolly, jostling scene before her, feeling the need to have her fellow human beings close by even if they were completely unaware of her neediness.

She walked along the River Arno. Was this the place where she'd fainted in her nightmare? She wasn't going to think about that. She'd seen a meme recently that had read, *Where attention goes, energy flows*. She'd just have to redirect her attention if she found it was straying to her past. And what better place to help her than Florence? If she couldn't find something to immerse herself in here then there was no hope for her.

So she found the exact spot where Julian Sands and Helena Bonham Carter had stood in the film, imagining his character George tossing the damaged photographs into the waters below. She then wended her way towards the Piazza della Signoria which she hadn't actually managed to see it on her first visit to Florence all those years before.

She walked up the steps into the loggia. She knew where she was heading. There was a very particular spot where Helena Bonham Carter as Lucy Honeychurch had sat in the film and Elise found it, sitting down and soaking in the view across the piazza. It was busy with tourists photographing the statues and the great hulk of the Palazzo Vecchio, once the residence of the Medici family. This truly was one of the most famous, historic and beautiful places in the world and she was right here in the middle of it. She allowed herself a moment of pure pride that she'd got herself here on her own. Gratitude too that life had allowed her to take this trip.

It was a curious thing, she thought – this need to see places with your own eyes. It wasn't enough that they existed or even that you could view them in photos or videos online. Nothing truly beat being there in person and Elise could see why now. Pictures were one-dimensional and could never truly evoke a response from the other senses. But it went beyond even the senses. It was the *feeling* of being somewhere beautiful that resonated the most – the effect that it had upon your heart. For the first time in an awfully long time, Elise stopped thinking. She found she was able to simply be and that was so wonderfully freeing.

After her morning of pure unadulterated sight-seeing, she found the loveliest little *ristorante* and ordered a huge bowl of pasta then treated herself to tiramisu, quickly realising how addictive this could become and how her waistline wouldn't survive a single week in Italy if she did this every day, let alone for a few months.

By the time she reached her apartment that evening, she felt fully sated with food, with beauty, with life. She pulled out the exquisite notebook she'd bought herself from the prettiest stationery shop she'd ever seen. The hardback cover was hand-marbled in swirling pinks and reds and the creamy pages inside were soft to the touch, inviting her to write. But what would she write? She didn't want to make a list of the places she wanted to see, nor did she really want to keep a journal of where she'd been. It had cost her far more than she'd ever spent on a single piece of stationery and she didn't want to waste it. It reminded her of the pressure of opening a brand-new exercise book in school and needing to make your handwriting extra beautiful on the first page.

Maybe she could just talk to herself and jot down whatever came into her mind.

And so she began to write.

You are going to have a wonderful trip.

She smiled at those first simple words – words she needed to hear and that nobody else in the world was going to tell her.

You are brilliant and resilient!

Elise laughed, liking the rhyme. Maybe it could be her new motto. If Florence could rise up after the extensive damage of the Second World War, surely Elise could survive a crabby old woman? The comparison made her smile, but she knew that the two couldn't really be compared. Emotional trauma could often take a lifetime to recover from – if at all. A city could be rebuilt in mere years.

You will have an adventure!

She frowned. Why had she written that? She hadn't come to Italy for an adventure. She'd just come to see things: the art and architecture – quietly and calmly in her own time. Still, that was adventurous enough. *Real* adventures were for other people, weren't they? And Elise Cherrington from a small town in the Midlands just wasn't the sort to have adventures.

CHAPTER TEN

Nuala had quickly realised that life on the road took on a new dimension. Time changed. Days didn't matter. She could rename them if she wanted to. Monday could be Market Day. Wednesday – Rest Day. Sunday – Fun Day. It really didn't matter. She'd even stopped looking at her map and Satnav on some days – just driving whichever way felt right. Stopping too. If a place was beautiful, she gave herself time to see it properly. There was no need to rush anymore. She didn't have a deadline and she didn't have to answer to anybody. That was particularly freeing. For the first time since she'd married, she didn't have to worry about Paul's reaction to what she wanted to do. She could be as eccentric as she wanted to be and she wouldn't have to witness his look of consternation if she suggested they visit a quirky museum or see a location from a favourite film. In short, she could do exactly what she pleased.

She was fast getting used to manoeuvring The Van although she still found pulling up in petrol stations and trying to find parking spaces in cities challenging. Reversing was also tricky, but she just gave herself plenty of time to get to places and tried not to feel flustered. After all, she didn't have to do any of this. It was meant to be fun, wasn't it? Nobody was forcing her to go on this adventure. In fact, her sister, Nora, kept trying to talk her out of it whenever they spoke on the phone, and she felt pretty sure Paul was furious with her for going through with it. She could just imagine what he was telling Saskia.

'She's devaluing one of our main assets!'

Well, this 'asset' was now her home and her vehicle to her future. *If* she managed to get used to it.

She'd read a good tip on a Van Life forum where somebody had a post-it note on their dashboard on which they'd written: "You are higher, wider and longer than you think!" Just in case they forgot.

There had been that time on the outskirts of Bath when she'd left her knickers on the roof of The Van to dry and had driven off with them still up there. They'd been good knickers too. She couldn't help wondering where they were now. Maybe a magpie had picked them up and now had a Liberty-print-lined nest. Anyway, she'd used it as an excuse to do a bit of clothes shopping. Now that Paul wasn't travelling with her, she was able to take up a little bit more space on the wardrobe front. Not that she wanted to overdo it. She liked the lighter capsule wardrobe she'd created for her travels. But it was hard to switch off that woman's gene of wanting to look pretty in new clothes and so she'd treated herself to a couple of summer dresses while in Bath.

She'd also made the decision to buy some wonderfully comfortable knickers. With the loss of her pretty little

Liberty knickers, she'd taken it as a sign from the universe to go big. And what a revelation it had been. Big comfy cotton knickers. These were the sort of knickers that a woman wore when she was quite sure nobody else would see them or else didn't give a damn about what they thought if they did. Her bottom was her own business.

She also ditched the last of her dreadful wired bras. She really didn't understand how she'd put up with them for so long. Well, she did. Paul liked them. But for the few minutes of joy he got from her wearing underwire bras, she'd endured years of agony. Who on earth had thought it was a good idea to put wire against soft flesh? And straps which dug into your delicate skin? Clasps too. Bras were nothing more than a modern torture device designed by men to keep women – as well as their boobs – in their place. Well, she wasn't having any of it and bought herself some wonderfully comfortable wireless and claspless bra tops. Okay, so they made her look as if she was wearing a kind of bandage, but she didn't care. She had other things on her mind like when was she going to pluck up the courage and actually leave the UK? So far, she'd been exploring the West Country and enjoying Exmoor, deciding not to go as far as Cornwall because she and Paul had had too many holidays there and she didn't want to be reminded of those days that now seemed like another lifetime.

She knew she'd have to leave the UK soon though. The longer she left it, the harder it would become. The main pull was that she genuinely wanted to explore Europe. That had been their plan – well, *her* plan – for years. France in particular had woven its spell over her ever since she'd taken a trip to Paris as a student. But it wasn't just the famous places she wanted to see like Paris and the Loire Valley. She wanted to see the provincial towns – the sort with a tiny bakery where you could buy your daily baguette, where old men played boules in a shady square and where nobody spoke English.

She'd always wanted to see the south of France too, but Paul hadn't been keen. Even though it was deemed a worthy location in terms of prestige, he'd thought it was too posy, too artificial. Plus, it was expensive. Too splashy. He didn't like splashy. He liked to keep things simple and quiet. So Nuala had gone along with his choices. But she could go there now.

'If I manage to leave the UK first,' she told herself as she navigated an alarming bend and then swerved around a pair of Exmoor ponies which were grazing by the side of the road. She stopped to film them for a new video, capturing the beauty of their pale muzzles and their shaggy dark manes and tails catching in the wind. She'd read that, while the ponies were able to roam freely across Exmoor, they were in fact owned by somebody. She wondered who these two belonged to and if the owners knew where they were. It was lovely that they were truly able to wander at will, but Nuala silently acknowledged that the thought of any animal belonging to her being left out in all weathers would definitely give her anxiety. It was a fine balance, she guessed – allowing something freedom while still taking care of it. Perhaps that was something she'd got wrong in her own life? Had she not allowed Paul enough freedom? Had she reined him in and forced him to trot along behind her? Well, he'd broken free of her now. And, in her own way, she'd broken free of him by taking The Van.

Her latest messages from him – both on her phone and

by email – had been furious. He was threatening to get the police involved, but she doubted very much that it was a police matter and didn't think he had the stomach to go down that route anyway. To be honest, she hadn't given any of it much thought. She knew she'd have to face things at some point – there were some issues that she couldn't avoid. Were they going to divorce? How would everything be divided? And where was she going to live? Would The Van become her permanent home long-term? Plenty of people lived in their vehicles and she'd seen that it could be a good life. But was it the right life for her?

As she watched the carefree ponies whose only thought was where their next mouthful of food was going to come from, she decided that she'd be more like them and try to live in the present moment. There was absolutely no point in worrying about the future. She was here now, on this beautiful moor with the day stretching out before her, full of wonders to be discovered, and she was going to embrace everything about it.

When Laurie woke up on her first morning at the yoga retreat, her eyes focusing on a colourful print of a hibiscus flower on the creamy white wall, she breathed a sigh of relief. She'd made it. She was here. She'd had the courage to make a decision on her own and she was going to reap the benefits of that.

The retreat was on the east coast of Tenerife – far away from the bright lights and Brits who flocked to the south-west corner of the island. She'd not seen much of her surroundings yet as it had been getting dark when she'd arrived and she couldn't wait to explore. The website had shown a beautifully landscaped garden with palm trees, cactus plants and bougainvillea. There was a pool and lots of outdoor seating in secluded nooks so that you could always finds a space of your own when you needed to simply just be. And oh how Laurie was looking forward to simply just *being*. She couldn't remember the last time she'd had that luxury. Her time had always been filled with other people's dramas and demands. But here she was with a whole week to stretch, breathe and meditate.

Of course, her time wasn't entirely free. There was quite the itinerary at the retreat. The morning meditation and yoga session began at eight thirty. Breakfast was at ten. There was a period of leisure from eleven until one when guests could use the pool and enjoy the gardens. Then a light lunch would be served before another meditation and yoga class. This was followed by an afternoon activity such as a visit to a local town, a walk in a forest or sea swimming.

Laurie couldn't wait to enjoy it all. This was the first time she'd taken a trip on her own since she was in her early twenties. She still remembered it vividly because everything had gone wrong from her forgetting to pack her camera to getting her handbag snatched on a street in Rome and then, the real cherry on the calamitous cake, missing her flight home. Maybe that's what had put her off going solo since then. Maybe that's why she'd chained herself to the dull predictable holidays with Jeremy instead of simply telling him that she was going to do something on her own. It was a pity she'd let fear clip her wings for so many years but she knew she wasn't alone in that.

For a moment, she thought of her work colleague Sally. Laurie had only spoken to her one more time before leaving.

'You're *retiring*?' Sally's eyes had widened in alarm.

Laurie had laughed, but then had felt bad because Sally had looked thoroughly gutted. It was as if she could see that Laurie had escaped and that she was being left behind – both at work and in the UK. Perhaps Laurie could send her a text. She picked up her phone, thinking she could nip outside and get a few photos and WhatsApp them to her, but she quickly thought better of it. It might just be rubbing things in. The sad truth was, Sally probably didn't want to hear from her again. Laurie would just be reminding her that she was daring to do something that Sally couldn't.

As she'd unpacked her suitcase the night before, Laurie had felt horribly guilty for being there and walking out on her job, her home, her family and friends. It made her wonder what exactly was she hoping to find here? Was there actually anything *to* find? What if it was all a huge disappointment and she got herself into a dreadful pickle like that nightmare trip to Rome? Or worse – what if she got *bored*? What if being on her own with all the time in the world wasn't all she'd dreamed it might be? Maybe that fear had also kept her prisoner over the years.

As she got washed and dressed for the first yoga session, she thought of all the hours people had taken from her over the years. Of course, there'd been an exchange: her time for money or her time for the wonders of motherhood. But she couldn't help feeling like a husk. She'd been existing as mere extensions of the people around her and had completely lost herself in the process. And yet, now that she was here on the island she'd so longed to get back to after the all-inclusive holiday with Jeremy five years ago, she had become fearful.

She took a moment to process this, looking in the mirror at eyes which had definitely lost their sparkle and skin that looked dull and time-worn. There were lines around her eyes and mouth that had slowly deepened over the years and probably not from excessive smiling. Her eyebrows were thinning and had to be drawn in these days and no amount of moisturiser seemed to make the difference it promised no matter what she spent on it. Time had definitely marched across her face and yet... there was something in the determined expression that willed her on. Her face might have lost its lustre, but a little peace and time in the sun could very well fix that. That was merely surface-deep, wasn't it? But the determination she could both sense and see was very evident. It was what had driven her to take a stand and it was what had brought her here.

She smiled at that. Ah, yes! A smile could fix everything. Her face suddenly lit up and she found her smile shifting into a playful giggle. When was the last time she'd giggled? She truly couldn't remember. She'd forgotten the feeling – the bright effervescence like champagne bubbles.

By the time she joined her first yoga session, she was in a much more positive frame of mind. There were ten students at the retreat and two teachers. There'd been a late get-together over supper the night before after everyone had arrived and they'd gone round the table introducing themselves and saying what they hoped to get out of the week. Laurie was one of four solo travellers there. The rest were couples. She'd felt a little twinge of envy at that – not because she wished Jeremy was with her. She could think of nothing worse than having his miserable face accompanying her to Tenerife. But she couldn't help wondering what it must be like to be part of a couple that did something like a yoga retreat together and to share the same interests and want to be together during a very special type of holiday.

On that first morning, they took yoga mats from the main studio out into the garden overlooking the swimming pool. It was already warm with a light breeze rustling the fronds of the palm trees above them. Laurie took it all in – the feeling of morning sun on her pale arms and the fact that she was in a T-shirt in early spring, the glassy quality of the air that came from being so close to the sea, and the sound of gentle chatter as everybody settled down on their mats. It was such a pretty sight with mats in every colour from hot pink to mystical purple. Everybody had dressed differently too. There was a mix of shorts, sweatpants and yoga pants. Laurie was wearing her favourite yoga pants in turquoise which always reminded her of the ocean whenever she wore them and made her feel slightly mermaid-like, which was no bad thing in a world which, for so many years, had felt distinctly unmagical.

She stretched her mermaidy legs out before her now as they warmed their limbs up with some simple movements, linking everything to the breath – that miraculous life force which was so easy to take for granted in a hectic world when breathing properly was so often ignored. But everything ultimately came back to the breath, didn't it?

That first day at the yoga retreat was wonderful. Breakfast was a sumptuous spread of bread, fruit and wholefoods after which Laurie had a swim before lying back on a sun lounger and letting her gaze float upwards into the palm trees. Their first outing had been into the mountains where they'd hiked through the pines, inhaling the clean scent of the trees and marvelling at the thin wisps of cloud as they climbed higher.

It amazed Laurie how quickly she adapted to her new routine at the retreat and she particularly enjoyed the morning yoga sessions. It felt so good to embrace gentle movement and breathwork at a time in the morning which was normally filled with anxious rushing to get to work on time. As Laurie stretched under the towering palms, the wind from the Sahara warm on her face, she could feel something awakening inside her. A kind of peace, perhaps. A peace that had been buried under years of noise and that she hadn't taken the time to nurture. It was funny to think of it being there all that time. Ignored but very much alive deep inside her. Like an eternal light in her darkest recesses that she could now allow to shine brighter.

After Jeremy had dropped her at the airport, she'd got herself through security and then gone into the toilets and cried silently for a good ten minutes. When she'd emerged, she'd studied her blotchy face in the mirror and done her best to calm her skin down with cold water. A teenager at the next sink stared at her.

'You okay?' she'd asked, her eyes squinting at her through her fake eyelashes.

Laurie had nodded. 'I'm okay.' She'd managed a weak smile at the youngster's kindness.

She thought about that small moment of kindness now as she sat on her yoga mat as their yogi guided them through a meditation. Her husband had been abrasive, distant and dismissive and yet this total stranger had been caring and concerned. Life truly was a mystery to her. And yet she was getting glimpses of something deep within herself as she spent time alone at the retreat.

She was beginning to realise that she was always looking for external validation – whether from her husband, her children, her boss or her friends. And this wasn't a new thing either. Even at school, she remembered her form tutor taking her to one side after an argument with her best friend Alison, which had led to a big bust-up. Laurie could still feel the sting of it all these years later.

Mrs Henderson had shaken her head.

'Oh, Laurie – you never have any confidence in your own capabilities – you always look outside of yourself. But it's all *inside*! You carry the strength within you. Don't look for it anywhere else. And certainly don't look for it from Alison Everett!'

It's all inside.

Laurie rolled those words around her mind now as their yogi chanted in a tongue that was foreign to her.

It was true – Laurie had never really belonged to herself. She'd always been somebody else's. Somebody's daughter, somebody's wife, somebody's employee. Well, it was time to reclaim herself. Only, it wasn't as easy or as simple as that. Her body seemed to be rebelling against her. It was twitching, itching, aching and straining. Perhaps because she had never really allowed it to be still before other than the brief yoga sessions she did at home. Was it any wonder that her body was protesting now that she was trying to force it to be still? It just wasn't used to it and kept fidgeting.

As the yogi continued to chant, Laurie gave herself a severe talking-to.

Will you relax, woman! You haven't got to be anywhere and you haven't got to do anything.

She remembered hearing a line in a film once: "Relax and the world is a beautiful place?" She really needed her body to be able to do that. She had tried to find ways of relaxing before. She'd once signed up for a yoga class in the draughty local village hall and she'd loved some of the stretches and moves, but she just hadn't understood all that breathwork and meditation stuff. Up one nostril and out the other? What was *that* about? Were we really meant to breathe that way? Maybe really stressed people needed that in order to slow down, but Laurie had hated being told when to breathe in and out. As for meditation – wasn't being out in nature enough? Walking, swimming in the sea, looking at a night sky packed full of stars?

And since when have you done any of that?

She sighed. Good point. When had she taken herself off for a walk that wasn't to the shops in a mad hurry to get ingredients for dinner? When had she last swum in the sea? When had she walked in the countryside simply for the pleasure of the scenery?

That's what this time at the retreat was about. It was a complete mind and body reset.

She shifted on her yoga mat again, cursing her body for not cooperating. Daring to open an eye, she glanced at the other attendees around her. Of course, they all appeared to be absolutely still and serene. How did they do that? Maybe they were retreat junkies and had more practice than her. She'd spoken to almost everybody now and had been relieved to find that they were all friendly. That had been one of Laurie's fears about travelling solo especially to a place like a yoga retreat. What if she felt isolated? What if there was nobody to chat to? Laurie wasn't a hugely gregarious sort of person, but she also didn't like feeling lonely and she loved a good conversation – something that had often been sorely missing in recent years with her children having left home and her husband forever hiding behind his newspaper.

So it was rather wonderful that she fell into step with

Kitty whilst out hiking in Teide National Park on the third day of the retreat. The younger couples had charged ahead and, although Laurie and Kitty were far from unfit, they also didn't have anything to prove to the world anymore and were both enjoying a slower pace, taking in the ochres and terracottas of the landscape and the extraordinary blue of the sky above Mount Teide.

Kitty was in her mid-seventies and had silver-grey hair tied up in a messy bun and a hairband in swirling purples framing her olive-skinned face. Her tanned arms were covered with jangling bangles which the yoga teacher had politely asked her to remove during class as the silvery tinkling sound they made every time she moved was slightly distracting. He'd also disapproved of the numerous silver and turquoise rings she wore but she'd refused to remove those, saying they were a part of her and that they probably wouldn't come off even if she made an attempt to remove them.

She'd been going to yoga retreats since retiring at sixty and did two or three a year – usually in southern Europe or the Canary Islands so that she could get her quota of sunshine at the same time.

'I should have retired much earlier!' she confessed to Laurie. 'Why do we put up with work? And don't get me wrong – I didn't even hate my job.'

'What did you do?'

Kitty sighed. 'I'm loathe to answer that question as it makes me wonder what I *really* did for all those years! But my job title was Marketing Manager. It just meant I pushed a load of admin around all day.' She shrugged. 'There were some fun projects, but it was still a desk job that sucked up *way* too much of my life.'

Laurie nodded in understanding and told Kitty a little about her own role and how relieved she'd been to leave.

'I try not to ask people what they do for a living these days,' Kitty confessed. 'Because it's such a small part of what makes a person. Now, I know a lot of people gain their identity through their work. Meaningful work that they've chosen. But so many of us simply fall into a job and end up getting stuck, and it seems wrong to put somebody in a box and see them through a lens that doesn't tell you anything about them in any sort of meaningful way.'

Laurie nodded in agreement. She'd never thought of it like that before, but it was often the first question that popped out of somebody's mouth when they were introduced to you.

'So what would you ask instead?' Laurie said as Kitty paused to take a photo of a mean-looking plant with lethal-looking spikes.

She looked thoughtful for a moment. 'Well, nothing that might land me with a restraining order,' she said, 'but something a bit more personal. Like...' she paused, 'If you can only make one more trip, where would you go?' She nodded. 'That's my favourite question.'

'And what would your answer be if I asked you that?'

'Antarctica, but it's beyond my budget. It's getting too crowded now these days too, isn't it?'

'I wasn't aware people were actually going there!' Laurie said, feeling hopelessly out of touch with everything.

'I might just go to Iceland instead although that's pretty expensive too. I guess that's why I keep returning to Spain and the Canary Islands. So, how about you? If you could only do one trip?'

Laurie smiled. 'I guess I'm doing it now. Although I'm

not really sure where I'm going. I'm just giving myself a chance to scratch a few itches.'

'And how does it feel?'

'Pretty good. It's early days so I'm still feeling guilty about being here.' She looked up at the towering rocks above them with their marvellous bulbous patterns. This landscape really had the power to put you in your rightful place and Laurie suddenly felt so small and vulnerable.

'It's normal to feel guilty when we're being good to ourselves,' Kitty told her. 'Why is that, do you think? It's crazy, isn't it?'

Laurie nodded. 'I think it's a woman thing. We spend so much of our lives in the role of caregiver and yet we often neglect ourselves.'

'You see – that makes me angry!' Kitty said with unexpected passion.

They talked for a while about how women were always expected to fall into that role. Kitty told her about her useless brother who, although living much closer to their parents, had never lifted a finger to help out when they'd became sick and frail. It had been Kitty who'd had to drop everything and travel back home to take care of them.

'And of course I did it willingly, but it did take its toll. I suppose that's why I'm allowing myself all of this now,' she said, motioning to the mountains and the great sky above them.

Laurie felt tears pricking the backs of her eyes and told Kitty about what had brought her to Tenerife – the soul-sucking job, the grey days in the UK, the stranger in the house that was her husband, and the unbearable weight of needing to find more in life. And Kitty never once interrupted her. She just listened with an occasional nod of her head and murmur of acknowledgement.

It was the first time Laurie had ever really opened up about her marriage and it felt wonderfully freeing. She'd never felt able to talk to anybody about it before. Her family all had their own issues and she'd never felt close enough to anybody at work to suddenly blurt out that she was unhappy with her domestic situation. She certainly hadn't been able to talk to her children about it – that would have been both selfish and inappropriate. So it was rather wonderful to tell Kitty about all her misgivings and insecurities as they walked into the strange, lunar-like landscape.

And maybe it was easy to talk to Kitty because she was a stranger and Laurie knew they probably wouldn't meet again after the week at the retreat. This was a safe space. Kitty didn't know the world Laurie came from. The two women only existed in the present moment. Their very separate worlds would collide for one week only and, in a way, that gave Laurie permission to be completely honest and not hold back.

'I feel like a layer of me is missing since menopause,' she confessed as they found a friendly rock to sit on. It was warmed by the sun and seemed to welcome them into the landscape. 'I'm so sensitive. I'm emotional all the time. The slightest thing will set me off.'

'Ah, I remember the joy of those heightened emotions,' Kitty said with sarcasm. 'The days when even commercials had the power to set me off! Especially those ghastly Christmas ones.'

'Don't they make everybody cry?'

'Apparently not!' Kitty said. 'But they could wreck me for hours when I was at my lowest ebb.'

Laurie smiled at that. 'Society writes us off, makes comedy sketches about us and dismisses us as done, but I don't feel done. Not yet.'

'You're a youngster!' Kitty told her which made Laurie laugh.

'Right!'

'Believe me!' Kitty went on. 'Do you remember your thirties?'

'Of course!'

'Well, you have as much time between your thirties and now as you have between now and the age I am.'

Laurie's mouth dropped open.

'Makes you think, doesn't it? How much happened during those two decades. All the emotions you had, the experiences – the life you led. Well, you have that same amount of time again and maybe a lot more beyond. You're fit and you have enthusiasm. So you're definitely not done, Laurie, believe me!'

Laurie didn't know what to say. It sometimes took an outsider to point something out to you and give you a perspective you just wouldn't have had on your own. Here she was thinking that her best years were behind her and that menopause and retirement were the beginning of the end. Even though she'd taken herself off travelling, she couldn't shake the feeling that she was merely staving off the inevitable and that she was in denial. At some point, she'd have to go home and sort out life with the man behind the newspaper. Then she'd wait for her children to give her grandchildren and the whole cycle would start again, wouldn't it? Grandma Laurie would once again be at the beck and call of others until her body finally gave way.

'You are *so* not done,' Kitty said again, as if she knew Laurie needed to hear it one more time.

'Unless Teide erupts,' Laurie said as she gazed up to the peak of the third biggest volcano in the world.

'Well, there is that!'

The two women laughed, cementing their friendship even if it was just a transitory one. They had gone deep and had made wonderful discoveries together and that was enough.

CHAPTER ELEVEN

After having the all-too-realistic nightmare that her mother was still alive, Elise had managed to settle into her new life in her Florence apartment. How quickly she had, she thought, and how far away England felt to her now. She didn't miss her home and she certainly didn't miss work. It had taken her a little while to break the routine of getting up at seven in the morning and leaving the house by eight thirty for a nine o'clock start at Bevington House. And her brain still hadn't quite switched off from those dreaded after-work visits to her mother's home, even though she hadn't had to do them for months now.

One afternoon, she treated herself to a drink and pastry at a lovely place overlooking a small piazza and glanced at her phone to check the time – not that she had anywhere to be – but old habits were hard to break. She really wished she hadn't looked because she immediately realised it was the time she used to leave work and head across town to her mother's place, and all the swirling emotions associated with those visits coursed through her system. It was a kind of emotional time travel that she didn't feel able to stop, no matter how much she willed herself back to the present moment in Florence with her beautiful pastry and her view of the pigeon-filled piazza. The past still had her in its clutches and could drag her back at any moment.

One thing had become quite clear since she'd been in Florence and that was she couldn't go on living in her home town. There was too much of the old Elise there and she could feel herself breaking free from her now that she'd put some space between her and her old life. In the very brief time she'd been in Italy, she could feel the shackles of the past had begun to loosen and it felt wonderful. But what that meant in practical terms, she couldn't yet answer. Would she need to find another job? Or could she commute if she moved? There were so many questions to find answers to and, to be honest, she didn't want to think of them now because they would drag her back to the UK and she really didn't want to go back there even if it was just in her thoughts.

She knew she had some big life decisions ahead of her and she knew that she was evolving and slowly finding a new Elise. That was exciting but it was also scary. There was no getting away from the fact that change was scary and one of the scariest things was that she was on her own in all of this. Her brother wouldn't want to be bothered with her insecurities and she wasn't close enough to any of her work colleagues. She was just beginning to realise what an isolated life she'd led for so many years. Her daily routine had consisted of her moving between the three locations of home, work and her mother's house.

But she was fully intent on making up for lost time now and the funny thing was that she didn't feel alone in

Florence. Was it the excitement of being in a city? She didn't think so. Was it the fact that she'd always been independent and hadn't relied on anybody else even if her solitary existence hadn't been completely by choice? She wasn't sure. One thing she was sure about was that she had two of the very best travel companions with her: her trusted copy of E M Forster's *A Room with a View* and her Great Aunt Clara's sketchbooks. During her first few days in Florence, Elise hadn't looked at either of them even though she'd been tempted oh-so-many times, especially in the evenings when she was back at her apartment. But she was quite determined to make her own memories in Florence and make her own special version of the city before she followed in the footsteps of others and saw it through their eyes. That was important to her.

Of course, she couldn't help but think of Forster's beloved characters as she walked around the streets and piazzas and visited the churches and the loggias. She had read the novel countless times and had seen the Merchant Ivory film adaptation even more times and could clearly picture Helena Bonham Carter in the Piazza della Signoria in that marvellous hat and Judi Dench flying around the backstreets in her dark cloak.

One place the characters of the novel didn't visit was The Uffizi Gallery – an unforgiveable act especially as they were in the city for a good length of time. It was very high on Elise's list of places to see and she'd done the sensible thing and booked skip-the-line tickets which saved the long queues for entry tickets on the day. In fact, she'd booked as early a ticket as possible in the hope of avoiding too many crowds as, along with the Accademia, it was one of the most popular places in the city.

The Uffizi was a vast building and it felt a little daunting to enter its labyrinthine corridors but wonderfully exciting too. It reminded Elise of when she'd arrived at Bevington House for her first day of work as custodian. She'd felt so completely overwhelmed and had wondered if she'd taken on more than she could cope with. What if she couldn't even find her way to her office? How could she hope to be in charge of such a huge collection if she got lost on the way to the staff toilet which happened – twice!

But Elise wasn't at work now and it didn't really matter if she got lost. Was getting lost even possible in a place like The Uffizi? With so much beauty to see, taking a supposed *wrong turn* would surely just introduce you to another wonderful sight.

However, there were certain pieces the museum was famous for and, like everyone, she wanted to see Sandro Botticelli's *The Birth of Venus*. What was it about some paintings that made them so famous and revered? And what made people need to see them with their own eyes? Why wasn't a reproduction in a book or a page online enough?

The painting had been commissioned as a wedding gift for a Medici cousin and so had been hidden away from the world for many years. It made you wonder just how much incredible art there was intended for private eyes only. As a custodian, Elise had long been aware of the selfish tendencies of the rich to collect all that was beautiful in the world. The collection she presided over included many fine paintings, sculpture and silver collected on "The Grand Tour" of Europe which previous owners had taken. There were also pieces the family had commissioned over the years from elaborate furniture to exquisite carpets. Some of the individual pieces could pay her annual salary. Some could possibly pay for her house.

She couldn't help wondering what the collection in The Uffizi was worth in terms of money and then dismissed the question as redundant. That wasn't why she was here.

So why are you here?

Her own question caught her a little off-guard. She was here to see the beauty of the world. To gift herself the time and joy to be a tourist, an observer, a student. She wanted to learn and to absorb. She wanted to follow in the footsteps of Great Aunt Clara. She wanted a release after the years of restraint. But, more than anything, she wanted to *feel* something. For so many years, Elise had been living in the shadows, a faint whisper of a person. She'd moved through her days feeling numbed – as if her senses had been dialled down and her thoughts repressed. Or maybe she'd done that to herself as some kind of defence mechanism. She wasn't totally sure. She just knew she'd been living a sort of half-life. But now it was time to step out of the shadows. She could finally feel the pull of life and she longed to participate in it fully.

Even though she'd been one of the first in the gallery, there was still a sizeable crowd paying their respects to the Goddess of Love and Elise joined them, standing in front of the fifteenth-century painting in awe, marvelling at everything about it: the shape of the shell, the paleness of Venus's skin and the feel of the wind moving through her hair. And her expression. It was at once tender and sensual.

Her eye was also drawn to the winds, Zephyr and Aura, in the top left of the painting. She loved the tangle of their limbs as, together, they blessed the new-born goddess with their breath.

Elise had read a lot of criticism about the painting especially about the central figure. Her proportions were all wrong. Her neck was too long and her pose wasn't realistic as she was leaning in a way that would have made balance impossible. Were the critics right? Could you really tell a goddess that her neck was too long and that her pose wasn't possible? Or was it a fault in the painter? Had Sandro Botticelli made these choices deliberately? And did any of it really matter? Elise glanced around at the other people who were jostling in front of the painting and wondered what questions were running through their minds if any at all. Did people pick paintings apart as they were looking at them or were they simply transfixed by the colours and shapes and beauty? Elise felt lucky to be there seeing it with her own eyes. This had been part of her dream for so long and, now that she was here, she didn't want to question anything. She just wanted to absorb.

Something in particular that struck her was that all four of the figures in the painting were barefoot. Elise glanced down at her own very sensible shoes. When was the last time she'd been barefoot other than in the shower and bed, of course? When had she trod lightly across the earth like a carefree goddess? What must that feel like? The practical part of her immediately answered with the word *cold*. Quickly followed by *dangerous*. Oh, to have a practical mind. She cursed herself now as she allowed her body to lean ever so slightly to the left in imitation of Venus.

Her custodian's eye noted the modest gold frame and was pleased that it didn't overwhelm the painting as frames often did.

As if the beauty of Venus wasn't enough for the senses to contend with, the room also contained Botticelli's other masterpiece: *Primavera*. Elise had a book with the painting on the cover but nothing prepared her for the beauty of the real thing. There was so much joy and movement and life in it. Elise loved the fruit trees and the flowers, and the diaphanous dresses worn by The Three Graces were quite spellbinding. As a viewer, you were almost invited into the scene – to dance barefoot among the flowers.

There was a feeling of a tapestry about it with its rich, dark colours still hinting at winter but which 'Primavera' or spring was fast supplanting. It reminded her of the passing of the seasons and that everything is ever-changing. Even the longest winter will be ended by the coming of spring. Elise took comfort in that.

She returned to *Venus* for one more blissful moment, a melancholy feeling coming over her because she knew this wasn't just the first time she'd visit it, but probably the only time. She brought her phone out of her bag, careful to attach it to her wrist with its lanyard. As a solo female traveller, she knew she had to take extra safety precautions as there was no back up if she dropped or lost her phone or had it snatched from her.

It was then that she became aware of a man watching her. He was standing just a little way off to her right. No, he wasn't watching her, he was *sketching* her. She turned, giving him her full attention and noticing the quick, slick movements of his pencil across the page of his sketchbook and the way he glanced up at her every few seconds, his dark eyes set deep in his tanned face. He looked Italian but he could be from any part of southern Europe.

She felt herself frowning as he realised she'd seen him and approached her still clutching his sketchbook.

'You are English, yes?'

She nodded slowly, instantly on guard.

'You know you look *exactly* like her!' he told her, his face lighting up. 'I can't believe it! Your skin. Your hair!' He waved his left hand around excitedly. 'Uncanny!'

Elise might not have ventured out into the world much and her knowledge of men was terribly limited for someone in their fifties, but she knew what a load of baloney sounded like. However much he tried to flatter her ego – for what woman wouldn't want to be told that she looked like the Goddess of Love who had been held aloft as the pinnacle of female perfection for over five hundred years? – It would be so very easy to succumb to his praise. But she wouldn't be taken in.

She looked down at his open sketchbook. He was talented, she'd give him that. He'd done a very good job of incorporating her features onto Botticelli's Venus and a part of her would have liked to have the sketch from him. But sense prevailed. This wouldn't be a free gift. In fact, she believed it to be some kind of scam. An artistic one might be a cut above those going on out in the streets, but a scam was a scam. Was it money he was after or something else? Elise wasn't about to find out.

But something did occur to her.

'May I see?' she asked.

He held his sketchbook up a little higher.

'No – may I...' Before he realised what she was doing, she had hold of his pad and quickly flipped through it. Sure enough, it was full of images of Botticelli's Venus. The pages before the sketch of Elise were full of others with dozens of women's faces inserted into Venus. Then, when she dared to flip the pages forward, she couldn't help laughing as she saw the man had page after page of Venus's image with the face left blank for him to sketch whoever might be standing in front of the painting next who took his fancy.

She glanced at him as he took his pad back.

'You have found me out,' he whispered and gave her a wink.

'Does this work for you with women?'

He gave a little shrug. 'Sometimes,' he said and then his eyes widened. 'But I see you are smart. I think we have a *lot* in common. How about I take you to lunch? I know a little place–'

'Perhaps,' she interrupted, 'you should go outside and sketch. You're good, but I think you're wasting your time in here drawing the same image over and over again. Doesn't that get boring?'

She could see his eyes had glazed over. He didn't want a lecture. He'd found the subject he wanted to draw and the talent he wanted to pursue and it had nothing to do with self-fulfilment or artistic passion. So Elise shrugged, mirroring his movement of a few moments earlier and left him to it. Sure enough, when she glanced back, he had turned the page in his sketchbook and was adding the eyes, nose and mouth of a different woman who was standing in front of Botticelli's masterpiece.

Elise spent another couple of hours in The Uffizi after leaving the Botticelli's – or maybe it was longer – she wasn't keeping track and that was part of the joy. She had nowhere else to be. She could take her time and spend the whole day here if she wanted. It would be easy to do – the place was enormous – a kind of palace of light and beauty. Even the ceilings were works of art, demanding her attention. It was hard to imagine that they had once been offices – for that was what the word 'uffizi' meant. These had been the offices of the grand Medici family whose actual palace – the Palazzo Vecchio – was next door.

She made her way to the first floor which, after the floor with the Botticelli's and the Da Vinci's, was much quieter. She could feel herself exhaling. Of course, there was a little bit of excitement around Caravaggio's *Head of Medusa* – dramatically pictured on a shield, her face frozen in horror at the moment of her execution.

After that Elise drifted, filling her vision with wonders until she could take no more and admitted defeat. If she had the time and the money, she would have happily returned again and again to see as much as she could, but there was more to Florence than The Uffizi as her friends in *A Room with a View* had discovered.

It was always a strange moment to leave the cocoon of a gallery or a museum and step back into the real world and Elise took a moment for her senses to adjust. There were still enormous queues to get in and she was glad that she hadn't left it any later in the day. She looked at the people in the queue as she walked by. Most were in couples. Friends, partners, family. The world moved in couples, didn't it? The thought made her wince for a moment, but she quickly shook off her self-pity because she felt completely content in her own company. She was doing exactly what she wanted, when she wanted to do it and, glancing at some of the faces in the queue, she imagined that not everybody was thrilled to be there. There was one particularly miserable-faced man who looked as if he might have been dragged there by his partner who was talking ten to the dozen as his eyes glazed over. Where would he rather be now, she wondered? That was the price of being in a couple, she thought – you sometimes had to compromise.

Elise allowed herself a little smile as she made her way to the nearest gelateria and bought a double scoop of pistachio ice cream. There was nobody to tell her that she shouldn't and nobody to reprimand her for eating dessert before she'd even thought about a proper lunch first. Her decisions – whether noble or naughty – were hers alone to make and for that she was truly grateful.

CHAPTER TWELVE

After her week at the yoga retreat, it was going to feel strange for Laurie to be on her own. For seven days, she had breathed and stretched and eaten and walked with this group of people. They had come together from so many different corners of the world and now they were dispersing. Only Laurie was staying in Tenerife and she knew that the place she was going to would be quite a rude awakening.

At breakfast on their last morning, she revealed her misgivings to Kitty.

'I'm not sure what I'm doing,' she confessed over the fruit platter. 'It's one thing to be solo within a group but I'll be completely on my own now.'

'You'll get into your stride,' Kitty said matter-of-factly. 'The trick is to remind yourself that travel is a privilege. Nobody is forcing you to do this. You've chosen it. And you can go home any time you want. Don't forget that.'

Laurie nodded as she helped herself to a pineapple ring. Kitty was right. It was a privilege to be here. She thought about

Sally at work and how fear had stopped her from leaving home. Laurie had already jumped that hurdle. It was probably the largest one too – getting out of the door. So why was she suddenly afraid now when the hardest part was already behind her?

'Any worries – just drop me a message,' Kitty added, obviously sensing Laurie was still feeling anxious. 'Or drop me a message anyway, okay? I don't have too many people interested in what I get up to on the road. It'll be good to have a solo travelling comrade.'

'Thanks, Kitty!' Laurie felt relief surging through her. Although they were parting ways, they could keep in touch. Laurie would have 'someone in the field' looking out for her. 'Where are you heading next?'

'Seville,' Kitty said. 'Then Cordoba, Granada, Ronda – that whole Golden Triangle in Andalucia. "Palaces and Paella", I'm calling it.'

'That sounds brilliant! I've got those places on my wishlist too.'

'Then you should definitely see them. Unless you're off to Morocco or somewhere else?'

'I'm afraid I've not planned very well. I kind of wanted to wing it but it's making me nervous now.'

'You'll be fine,' Kitty assured her. 'A few months on the road and it'll all seem like second nature.'

Laurie just couldn't imagine being on the road for a few months, but that's exactly what she'd intended to do – maybe taking the odd job here and eke out her redundancy pay. The reality was finally beginning to hit her though. She'd had this first glorious week in the safe bubble of the yoga retreat in wonderful company and with all her meals prepared for her and activities and excursions arranged by others. Now she was stepping into the unknown and it was all on her to organise it.

'How do you do it?' Laurie blurted out.

'Do what?'

'Everything!'

Kitty laughed. 'Because I want to. And I always ask myself, what's the alternative? I'm not the kind to stay at home and join committees or bake cakes for local fetes. I need a bit of excitement. A bit of uncertainty. Even if that makes me nervous. That's the stuff of life, isn't it?'

They finished their breakfast and helped clear the plates away and then the goodbyes began. The organisers were dropping people off at the airport and Laurie would be catching a bus from there to her next destination. She was absolutely dreading it.

'One day at a time,' Kitty told her as they said their final farewells at the airport. 'One *moment* at a time – we've learned that this week, haven't we? It's all about the present moment, right?'

'Right!'

'So you don't have to hold a whole trip in your head at once. Just work out what you need in the *here and now* and you'll have a fabulous trip.'

They embraced and it was such a warm and heartfelt moment that Laurie felt tears in her eyes. Then came the painful part of watching Kitty walking away, her backpack securely on as she headed into the airport, and Laurie wanted to run after her.

Take me with you!

But Kitty wouldn't want that. And would Laurie want that either? They had their own very separate solo adventures to have. It was one of the reasons she was here in

Tenerife – not just to see something of Europe at last but to test herself and see what she was capable of, and you couldn't really do that if you were with somebody else. You had to do it alone.

So Laurie watched as Kitty disappeared into a throng of tourists heading into the terminal. She was off on another adventure now, but so was Laurie.

She pulled her notebook out of her handbag. She could do the easy thing and hop in a taxi but that was expensive and she also wanted to start working things out for herself. She'd written a few notes down before leaving home and was pretty sure she knew what she was doing. There were buses every twenty minutes and the ride was under half an hour. She had no excuses not to do this. So, taking a deep breath, she picked up her backpack and went to find the bus stop.

After the peace of the retreat tucked away in the hills of east Tenerife, the all-inclusive hotel in Los Cristianos on the south-west coast was noisy, ugly and crowded. Laurie had booked it because it was cheap. Well, cheap for Tenerife. Nowhere was really cheap because you were up against so many other people wanting that perfect climate all year round. There weren't really low seasons in Tenerife and very few bargains. If there were bargains, Laurie hadn't been able to find any. So she'd chosen the three star hotel which turned out to have fifteen floors of family-filled rooms, a large and loud canteen and a swimming pool that was full of inflatables and surrounded by beer-swilling Brits.

It's a good location to be in. It's a good location to be in.

That's what Laurie kept chanting to herself. Los

Cristianos had a harbour from where she could take boat trips to La Gomera as well as daily trips to see dolphins and pilot whales. There were also many booking agents in the town which would allow her to see more of the island on day excursions. She would hardly be in the hotel at all and she had a pair of trusty ear plugs to shield her from any noise, including the nightly entertainment.

She'd known her budget wouldn't allow her to travel in five or even four-star style, and that was fine. It would be good for her to see different places although she had vowed to herself that she wouldn't ever do an all-inclusive hotel again after her and Jeremy's previous visit to Tenerife. That hotel was just down the road from where she was now and she remembered her frustration at how her husband would only leave the complex to walk into town. Even then, they hadn't had so much as a light lunch because he refused to spend a single penny on food when he'd already paid for full board. But Laurie wasn't going to live by such inflexible rules. This was a long-awaited holiday and, if she saw a restaurant she liked the look of, she was jolly well going to eat there.

After a somewhat restless night despite the ear plugs, Laurie woke early, attempted some yoga in the cramped space between her bed and the wardrobe and then headed into Los Cristianos. She was so excited to find a booking agent to book her first week's excursions. She looked at posters and picked up leaflets and had already done a good amount of research online. In short, she wanted to see *everything*. This was an island for those with an adventurous spirit as you could jet ski, paraglide or take a trip off-road in a buggy. But perhaps she'd book a couple of coach trips first, she thought – break herself in gently.

Only, when she walked into the agents she'd chosen and caught the eye of the guy behind the counter, she heard herself blurt out, 'I want to book the paragliding!'

He beamed her a smile. 'Great! When were you thinking?'

'As soon as possible – before I bottle out.' She nodded, as if reassuring herself. She needed to do this before she could think of excuses not to and, if she got into a safe routine of coach trips and sunbathing on the beach, it might never happen.

'You just got here?' he asked.

'Yes. Well, I've been at a yoga retreat on the other side of the island.'

'And they've let you out for good behaviour?'

'Something like that.'

They got on with the necessary paperwork and Laurie made the most of the booking agent's knowledge of the island, asking lots of questions about the best excursions to see as much as possible.

'You know, a lot of people leave the paragliding until the final day of their holiday,' he revealed.

'Really? Why?'

He cleared his throat and looked a bit anxious – as if he'd said too much. 'Oh, you know – in case anything goes wrong.'

Laurie gasped. 'You think I should put it off?'

'No, no! You'll be going up with the best – world champions, they are. Nothing to worry about.'

'Oh, good!'

'And booking it right away gives you a chance to do it again if you want to!'

Laurie gave a nervous laugh.

'You'd be surprised how many repeat customers we have. Once you get a taste for it, there might be no stopping you.'

Laurie smiled, trying to imagine herself being reborn as some kind of daredevil. Maybe she could be a poster girl for the menopausal adventurer.

Feel a hot flush coming on? Go scuba diving to cool off!

'The driver will pick you up outside your hotel tomorrow – details here. They'll ring you early in the morning if weather conditions aren't good but the forecast is looking fine at the moment.'

'Does it often get cancelled?'

'Not often,' he assured her. 'But you're here for a while, right? We can book you in again if need be.'

Half an hour later and Laurie had a heap of tickets and brochures for her booked excursions for the week ahead. It was tremendously exciting but rather nerve-wracking too.

You're doing it! You said you would and you're doing it!

She took a deep breath and allowed herself a moment to bask in all the feelings she was having – joy, trepidation, pride, peace. She wanted to celebrate but it was too early to do it with wine so she nipped back to her hotel and got her swimming bag ready because there was another little challenge she'd set herself for her time in Tenerife.

She caught the bus. She was really getting used to this independence thing now, she thought with a smile. It was so liberating to make a decision and follow it through without having to consult anyone else.

When she arrived, she almost lost her nerve and went for a long lunch instead, but she knew she'd regret it if she bottled out. So she walked to the beach and opened her bag, retrieving the travel towel she'd bought especially for her trip. It was lightweight and compact and dried very quickly, and it was to be her home for the rest of the day, she determined. Or at least until she'd got the beginnings of a good tan.

It was a beautiful sandy beach flanked with red and rugged cliffs. The sea was a dramatic blue but the waves were coming in at quite a pace and looked a little too rough for Laurie's liking. Still, she wasn't here primarily for the swimming. She was here for the experience because this was Laurie's first visit to a nudist beach.

Glancing up and down the length of the beach as casually as she could, she saw that there were all sorts here. Big people, slim people, men and women, couples and solos, sunbathers and swimmers. And most of them looked totally unfazed by the whole nude thing. It was normal, after all, wasn't it? It was only humans who made the whole nude thing an issue. Animals didn't feel the need to cover themselves up, did they?

Still, this was alien territory to Laurie. She'd never so much as sunbathed topless in her own garden and never even walked around the house naked. Jeremy would be appalled at the thought of her here, but he was never likely to find out. Laurie had only sent him the briefest texts to let him know she was okay and she certainly wasn't about to share her more risqué antics with him.

She didn't know anyone here, she told herself. Nobody cared who she was or whether she was clothed or not. This was one place where she wouldn't be judged. Although there was a man in dark sunglasses who she swore was eyeing her up from under a red and white parasol. She'd make sure she had her back to him.

Quickly applying sunscreen to her arms and legs ahead of taking off anything too revealing right away, she very nearly lost her nerve. But then she remembered the promise she'd made to herself over and over at the kitchen sink, at the coffee machine at work, at the bus stop, at the supermarket check-out – the promise to be brave, to challenge herself and to really live life to the fullest!

And those promises had brought her here – to this moment on the nudist beach where she could challenge herself: have adventures and do things she'd never done before whether that was paragliding or sunbathing naked on a public beach.

With that in mind, she took her clothes off.

But left her money belt on.

CHAPTER THIRTEEN

Nuala had finally made it to France and couldn't help feeling very pleased with herself. She'd crossed at Folkestone via the Eurotunnel to Calais, boarding Le Shuttle. It had been very exciting driving onto the train and she'd remained in her vehicle for the thirty-five minute crossing, trying not to think of the weight of water pressing around the tunnel. It was a surreal experience. The carriage she'd driven into was just one-vehicle deep and the yellow lighting gave it a slightly sinister feel as did the constant hum. She put some music on to distract herself.

It had been a great relief to see daylight again and thrilling to be in a different country at last and to leave the UK and all that it now represented in her mind. To celebrate, she'd found the nearest patisserie and bought a baguette and a tarte au citron, just imagining what Paul would say at the carb overload. Well, he wasn't here to chastise her. In fact, she'd taken a peek at his Facebook page and seen he was currently in Brighton with Saskia. Was that still considered Dirty Weekend territory? The weather had certainly looked filthy. There was a photo of them on the shingly beach together, a veritable storm howling around them. Serves them right, Nuala thought, as she'd peered closely at Saskia's creamy complexion and her too-bright lipstick. Blimey, she looked young.

She wondered what they'd been up to there and then immediately regretted her train of thought because she really didn't want to know. But she couldn't get over the thought that Paul had never taken *her* to Brighton. Why was that? She did, however, get a perverse sort of pleasure from the fact that she was still very much in his mind because he'd been texting her while he was there. In fact, he hadn't stopped texting her since she'd done a runner with The Van. The irate messages were piling up and, even though she'd deleted many of them, she knew she couldn't ignore them for much longer.

Now that she had crossed the English Channel and was a good chunk of the way across France, she at least felt a little safer. He wouldn't come after her, would he? He might threaten to – in fact, one of his messages had said he was on his way – but how could he be when he didn't know where she was? Not for the first time, she thanked her lucky stars that she had her own bank account rather than a joint one so that he wouldn't be able to trace her that way. He must just be trying to scare her into submission. Well, it wasn't going to work. She was well on her way now and had no plans to go back to the UK.

It was a wonderful feeling to have made it to France. Mainland Europe. The possibilities of where she could go overwhelmed her. Head north and she could explore Belgium, The Netherlands and even Scandinavia. Head east and she could venture into Germany. But she was heading south. To Paris.

Nuala didn't want to spend long in the capital as she knew she'd just make herself miserable seeing all the embracing couples in the most romantic city in the world, and she'd inevitably dwell on the trip that she and Paul had taken there. They'd been in their early twenties and had done it as cheaply as possible, staying on the outskirts and commuting in. They'd seen all the famous sites: the Eiffel Tower, Notre Dame, Sacré Coeur and The Louvre. Now, Nuala simply wanted to wander – to walk along the banks of the River Seine and pause on its bridges. To take a boat trip, to find streets of artisan shops and nibble on a croissant and sip a coffee. She didn't want to have to buy a ticket or queue for any hugely popular site. She was just going to drift around.

Of course, taking The Van into the centre of Paris wouldn't be possible. She wasn't sure what parking would be like, but she certainly didn't fancy finding out nor negotiating the roads with the impatient local drivers. So she parked up at a campsite on the outskirts and found her way to the nearest metro station. It was pretty straightforward, but it was the first time she'd been parted from The Van for any length of time and it felt strange leaving it. Would it be okay? Would *she* be okay? It might feel odd actually being out in the open for a whole day without its walls and home comforts around her. She'd got so used to parking up and just nipping into the back to sit down with a cup of tea or take a nap whenever she needed. And, of course, she had her own bathroom – a distinct advantage to travelling in The Van and something she always got a little anxious about when out and about in a city because you never quite knew what horrors awaited you when it came to finding a public toilet. But it would do her good to get outside. Van life was fast turning her into a hermit.

And she was so glad she'd made the decision to see Paris – if only for one day. It was good to walk after all the recent driving and Nuala covered a fair few miles as she took photos and film of the River Seine, getting some B-roll – some extra footage – for future YouTube videos. So far, she'd done most of her filming in The Van or at least near it when she was on her own, but it was quite a different thing to film in public – especially if she wanted to talk to the camera. She'd been slowly growing in confidence doing that – in the privacy of The Van. Now, with dozens of people hurrying by and jostling to get the same shots that she was trying to get, Nuala found herself losing her nerve. Maybe she'd just get a few shots without any commentary.

For a few hours, she lost herself in the beauty of the city. The spring light on the water, the trees wearing fresh new foliage. She strolled by the River Seine, marvelling at the great hulk of Notre Dame and thinking of its incredible restoration after the catastrophic fire. It was a real lesson in life, clearly telling her that destruction isn't the end of a story if you are willing to rebuild.

From there, she walked to the Jardin du Luxembourg, doing her best to focus on the fountains and statues rather than the couples strolling arm in arm or sitting on benches sharing a picnic.

It was while she was sipping coffee outside one of the boulevard cafés she'd dreamed of that she suddenly slipped into melancholy. All the couples around her were finally taking their toll. It wasn't just the romantic ones – even though there were plenty of them walking along hand in hand – but there were also friends laughing together, work colleagues chatting, a mother and toddler sharing ice cream. Everyone seemed to have *somebody* else. Except Nuala. Of course, there were other single people around her but her mind had dived into misery and she didn't allow herself to acknowledge them. The world moved in pairs. Pairs in Paris. Even those two words were anagrams of each another, she couldn't help thinking, making herself even more miserable.

What was she doing here? What was this mad idea of hers to take off to France and beyond *on her own*? She was obviously having some sort of crisis after Paul walking out on her. A moment of midlife madness. She wasn't going to berate herself for it – not after what she'd been through. She'd needed a release and so she'd done the only thing she could – run away. Or rather, driven away. Paul had left her no choice. He'd taken the car, their home had been sold and she was on her own. And she'd relished that moment of rebellion and the feeling that she could make her own decisions and didn't actually *need* him.

But it couldn't go on. She couldn't really drift around Europe on her own pretending to be happy because she was crumbling inside. She'd foolishly thought that driving a few hundred miles might cure a broken heart and that filling her days with sight-seeing would distract her from the fact that her world had fallen apart.

Finishing her coffee, she came to a realisation. She'd have to admit defeat and go home – even if The Van was her home at the moment. She'd have to take her home *home*.

She left the café, her heart aching. This wasn't exactly the image of herself that she'd had in mind for her special day. So much for the promised *joie de vivre* of Paris. Was this what happened when she left the safe cocoon of The Van?

Had she been hidden away in it for too long, obstinately rejecting reality?

After allowing herself one last moment of indulgence in a very elegant and expensive patisserie, Nuala headed out of Paris and back to the campsite. There was no need to rush anything. She would spend the night and take her time driving back to Calais. It seemed a shame to have finally made it to France only to turn back, but that couldn't be helped. At least she *had* made it this far. That counted for something, didn't it? She'd had the courage to do that at least instead of waiting for Paul to boss her around and sell The Van before she'd had a chance to enjoy it.

Paul.

She was going to have to ring Paul, wasn't she?

But not before scoffing the pastries she'd treated herself to. One last glorious moment of freedom before facing grim reality.

After enjoying every last crumb and then sweeping up the flakes that had fallen like confetti around her, she picked up her phone. Her stomach was churning with nerves, but she had to get this over and done with. Paul needed to know that she wasn't going to be a pushover and that he didn't have the right to make demands when he'd been the one to walk out on their marriage. But she also needed to let him know that she was coming back so they could sort things out.

However, she still didn't feel ready so she put her phone down and reached inside her handbag for her lipstick. It was silly really but she felt better with a slick of pink. Maybe it was a kind of warpaint. It didn't matter. As long as she felt prepared even if she wasn't going to physically show her face. She wasn't ready for one of those calls yet. She hadn't seen him since he'd walked out of their home after the infamous car boot sale. But there was a part of her that still missed his boyish face and that freckled nose she used to kiss last thing at night before falling into a peaceful sleep beside him.

She closed her eyes. She hadn't really known who she'd been sharing her bed with for all those years, had she? She'd never suspected he'd be capable of deceiving her.

He didn't deceive you. He just fell out of love with you and in love with someone else.

'Shut up!' she told her more reasonable self. 'He's a liar and a cheat! And now he's trying to steal my money.'

You don't know that. You're making assumptions.

'Maybe. But I bet I'm right.'

Talk to him. He's still your husband.

'Is he?'

She waited for a reply from her more reasonable self but none was forthcoming.

'Gotcha!' she said.

Oh, this was ridiculous, arguing with herself. What was she going to be like talking to Paul if she couldn't even agree with herself?

There was only one way to find out so she picked up her phone again and rang his number.

'Where the *hell* have you been?' Paul's voice barked a second later. He must have pounced on the phone the minute it rang.

'Well, I'm fine, thank you very much!' she responded lightly, determined not to let him rattle her so early in the conversation she was attempting to have with him.

'Did you get my messages? Why haven't you been in touch? Where *are* you? And where's the bloody van?'

She waited a moment before answering. 'France.'

'What?'

'I'm in France.'

The next few words out of his mouth weren't polite ones.

'In the van?'

'Of course in The Van! What did you expect me to do, Paul? We sold the house and you drove off in the car. I was homeless! And jobless, don't forget!'

'That was your decision, Nuala!'

'Yes, and I don't regret it.'

'You know you've devalued the van by leaving the country! You shouldn't even have driven it out of town. I could have got us a good deal. I've spoken to the dealership and I can probably fudge it as long as you've not put too many miles on the clock.' He paused. 'Nu?'

'What?'

'How many miles are on the clock?'

'I have no idea.'

'Well, take a look!'

Sighing, Nuala made her way to the front seat, dreading the reveal that was coming. 'Erm...'

'What is it?'

'Eight-fifty.'

'What?'

'It's eight hundred and fifty miles. Well, eight hundred and fifty-three if you want to be absolutely precise.'

A stream of expletives left his mouth and Nuala held the phone away from her ear, quite sure that her neighbours on the campsite would be able to hear him.

'What were you thinking? Is the van okay? You haven't scratched it?'

'The Van is fine.'

An icy silence fell between them and Nuala heard a voice in the background.

'Is that her?' she dared to ask.

'You do realise how irresponsible you've been, don't you?' Paul said, ignoring her question. In fact, he completely ignored everything she said after that. Instead, he was giving her a list of things she needed to do to keep The Van in as near-perfect condition as possible.

'This is so annoying, Nuala. I shouldn't have to do this but you've forced me to. We'll lose thousands on the van after your stupid stunt. I should have known you couldn't be trusted.'

And on he went – ranting and cursing.

It was when he referred to Nuala as 'a child' that something turned inside her. She'd genuinely been about to tell him that she was heading back. That he needn't make a fuss. That she'd come to her senses – well, maybe she wasn't going to admit that bit to him. But everything became clear to her. She couldn't go back. If she did, she would lose the momentum she'd built up so far on her journey. She might only have made it to Paris so far, but she'd come such a long way *inside*.

So she'd had a little wobble at the café. A wobble was normal. You could come back from a wobble. But it didn't need to decide the trajectory of your life. You didn't have to follow through if a decision you'd made was so obviously the wrong one.

'Nuala – tell me when you'll be back,' he shouted.

She took a deep breath and then she spoke calmly and clearly. 'I'm not coming back, Paul.'

There was that icy silence again.

'Did you hear me? I said I'm not coming back.'

'You're kidding me, right?'

'No.'

'That van is mine as much as it is yours.'

'And what do you think my lawyer will say about that when I explain how you left me in the lurch?'

'You've got a lawyer?'

She swallowed hard. It wouldn't do him any harm to believe that she'd got somebody fighting her corner but Nuala had never been a good liar.

'Not yet, but I'm thinking about it. I've got to look out for myself now.'

'Nu – listen – we can work this out. We don't need lawyers involved. You know how much that would cost. We can work this out between us. You just need to listen to me and come back.'

'Well, you see – I don't like that option. It really doesn't work for me. I spent years planning this trip and I'm jolly well going on it.'

'You can't be serious. You can't do it alone!'

'But I *am* doing it alone! And I'm doing it beautifully too. I was in Paris today. Remember you promised we'd always go back together? Well, so much for promises! Anyway, I went on my own and I walked along the Seine and I saw all the things I wanted to see and it was wonderful!' She carefully omitted telling him about her little wobble. 'I'm enjoying myself and I'm not going to stop. This is what I've worked so hard for over the last few years. My plans, my dreams, my money – I'm not handing those over to you so don't ask me to.'

He didn't respond for a moment.

'Did you hear me?'

'I heard you,' he said. 'I'm thinking.'

She closed her eyes. She could hear him breathing all the way from Brighton and it made her intensely sad that there was not only that physical distance between them but a huge emotional one now too.

'Well, okay,' Paul said at last.

'What do you mean?'

'You can do your trip. Just not in the van. Bring it back, we'll sell it and you can buy a more suitable one with your share of the money.'

'Oh, really? And by more suitable, you mean smaller?'

'Well, of course *smaller*! Half of that van is mine and it's ridiculous that you should be driving it around Europe on your own. You don't need all that space now that I'm not with you. That great double bed for starters. You don't need that!'

Nuala's mouth dropped open in shock at his assumption.

'Oh, so you're sleeping on your own in a single bed now, arc you?'

'Don't be petty.'

'You expect me to downsize and become celibate, is that it?'

'I'm asking you to be reasonable.'

'Just like you were when you walked out on me just before we were about to go away together?'

'There's no need to rake all that up again.'

'I think we're done here,' she told him, doing her best to remain calm while silently seething inside.

'Don't make me hire a private detective to find you, Nu!'

Nuala knew he was bluffing. He was too mean to pay for one.

'What good would that do?'

'I'm calling the police.'

'To tell them what? That the wife you walked out on is on holiday in her own van?' She laughed.

The volley of expletives that followed burned her ears and she hung up and turned her phone off. She refused to engage with him anymore. He wasn't playing fair and he wasn't even being reasonable – or polite.

She paced the small space of The Van, wishing she had someone to turn to – someone she could talk to. But she didn't. Other than her parents and sister, nobody even knew Paul had left her and would they care if they did? Couples broke up all the time. It wasn't really news and people had their own problems. They might sympathise for a moment, but then they'd move back to their own lives and rightly so.

But Nuala did have someone to talk to, didn't she? Her YouTube viewers. They might not be great in number, but they had been wonderfully supportive so far. Many had left questions in the comments wanting to know more about her situation. Some had left wonderfully kind messages of support and encouragement. Others had left incredible stories about their own midlife stories and how their lives had changed out of all recognition.

Before she could stop to question whether this was a good idea or not, Nuala turned her phone back on. Her hair was a mess and she was wearing her favourite old jumper with the hole in the right shoulder, but she wasn't thinking about any of that. She was mad and she needed to vent.

And vent she did.

CHAPTER FOURTEEN

When her alarm clock woke her up, Laurie groaned and wished she didn't have to get out of bed. She'd finally got to sleep some time after two in the morning after someone on her floor had made a very loud, very drunken progress down the entire length of the corridor, banging on random doors as they tried to locate their room.

Swinging her legs out of bed and pushing her hair out of her eyes as she found her slippers, she walked towards the window. There was a chance that the paragliding might be cancelled but, when she drew the curtains back and saw how still the palm trees were, she knew it was probably going to go ahead.

What had she been thinking? She couldn't throw herself into the air. Maybe she should cancel, only she knew she wouldn't get her money back at this late stage, and she hated wasting money. Maybe she'd just get in the pickup car, head up into the hills and watch everyone else. They couldn't make her do it, could they? She could say she didn't feel well or something. She'd just hang back and take photos. And she could always pretend she'd done it if anyone asked. She shook her head. Deception wasn't her thing. She could never take credit for something she hadn't done.

Pulling herself together, Laurie showered and dressed, ate her all-inclusive breakfast and was outside waiting for her pickup in good time. When the Land Rover pulled up a moment later, Laurie found she was the only one to get in, but the young driver told her they were picking up a family of four from Costa Adeje. Laurie was glad to have their boisterous company a few minutes later. The mum, Pippa, leaned forward from the seat behind and chatted to her.

'I can't believe you're doing this on your own!' Pippa confided, making Laurie feel a little braver than she had when she'd got up that morning.

'I can't believe it either.'

'Do you have family?'

'Yes!'

'And what do they think?'

'Well, my husband – he isn't *totally* supportive of the idea.'

'Well, you go for it! We just get the one life, right?'

Laurie nodded. 'And we shouldn't have to wear somebody else's handcuffs.'

Pippa laughed. 'That's a very good way of putting it!'

The Land Rover headed into the mountains, winding up narrow roads that didn't look as if any tourist had ever driven along them. It was a strange landscape – not beautiful. A bit scrubby and scruffy. Laurie started to feel uneasy. Maybe they'd been kidnapped and were being taken to some hideout and Jeremy would be asked for an extortionate ransom. The thought made Laurie both anxious and amused because she had a feeling that he'd refuse to pay.

Though she told herself not to be silly, she was still relieved when, a few minutes later, they pulled into a gravel parking area where there were other people. They weren't being kidnapped.

'Leave everything in the vehicle,' the driver told them. 'Bags, hats, sunglasses.'

'Can I wear my money belt?' Laurie asked.

'No. Nothing can get in the way of the harness. Everything will be safe in the car.'

Laurie's anxiety returned as she removed everything that was to be left in the Land Rover. As a solo female traveller, she hadn't been parted from her money belt, purse or phone. She watched the family as they organised themselves. If she wanted to jump, she was going to have to follow the rules.

The launch area wasn't what Laurie had been expecting. It was a steep slope covered in Astroturf. There were about a dozen instructors present and everybody introduced themselves. Laurie found herself partnered with Carlos from Madrid who had left the city as soon as was able to and had been paragliding since he was fifteen. Now in his forties, he looked healthy and safe, Laurie thought with relief, because she was about to entrust him with her life.

He excused himself for a moment and she saw him reach for his phone. Suddenly feeling a little lost and alone, Laurie turned to the family she'd travelled up with who were standing behind her.

'I wonder what we're waiting for,' she said to Pippa. She was anxious to get going as quickly as possible before she changed her mind again.

'They're calling colleagues down on the coast – checking what the weather's like down there. It might be good where we are, but that's the direction we're heading in.'

Laurie nodded. That made sense.

'They're watching the waves too – white horses might mean trouble.'

'And we don't want trouble at a thousand metres, do we?' Laurie said with a nervous laugh.

'Absolutely not!'

'Have you done this before?' Laurie asked, thinking Pippa sounded knowledgeable.

'Last year. Had our first holiday here and we were hooked.' She edged a little closer to Laurie. 'But it gets a bit expensive when there are four of you and nobody wants to miss out. Solo travelling definitely has its perks!'

And with that, Carlos was off his phone. 'Laurie – let's get you ready.'

A few moments later, she was wearing her helmet and harness. It all felt very insubstantial. Was this really going to keep her airborne?

'Is there a back-up parachute for me?' Laurie asked.

'No need.'

Laurie tried not to show her alarm at this news and she glanced behind at her instructor one more time. He looked fine of course. She was being paranoid. Nothing was going to happen to him healthwise in the next half hour. She hoped.

'You are strapped to me. You'll be safe.'

She nodded. Her mouth had gone horribly dry.

'We will be running towards the windsock. You will feel a tugging behind you, but don't look back! Keep moving forward, okay?'

'Okay!'

'Whatever you do, do *not* sit down! Keep moving, okay? Towards the windsock.'

'Okay,' she said again. 'Windsock, yes!'

'Do *not* sit down until I tell you!'

She nodded, hoping it was all going in and that she wouldn't let either herself or Carlos down. Oh, dear. Those nerves were kicking in again and the sea looked an awfully long way off as did the ground below the mountain. They were a long way up here. But that's what she'd paid for.

He handed her a long black stick with a GoPro camera at the end of it. She tried to contain her surprise. She hadn't factored in that she'd be holding on to anything other than the straps attached to the parachute.

'Don't worry, it's all tied together,' Carlos told her as if reading her mind. 'You want pictures, no? And video? Proof you've done this!'

Laurie nodded. Pictures and video would be fun and, like he'd said, *proof*.

She wasn't sure how long they stood there, joined together, the red parachute on the ground behind them waiting for its moment of glory, but it wasn't long.

'Okay, *go*! Run, run, run! Don't look back.'

Laurie ran – or rather, she attempted to run but didn't feel like she was getting anywhere because of the enormous dragging sensation behind her.

'Run, run, run!'

And then they were up and Carlos was pulling her down into the strange harness seat.

'Woo-hoo!' he cried and Laurie laughed. They were up and already high off the ground, the red parachute open above them. Laurie held tightly onto the GoPro handle with her right hand and the strap of the parachute with her left. The wind pushed against her face. It was a lot noisier than she'd imagined as they moved through the air. Their speed was something she hadn't expected.

'Okay Laurie?' Carlos called from behind her. 'Smile for the camera!' He took the stick from her and whizzed it around, getting stills and film from all sorts of creative, fun angles. Laurie smiled, laughed and whooped. She felt like a child.

They had left the mountains behind them and she glanced back. What a sight! They were flying high above roads and fields, heading towards the sea, and she could see the island of La Gomera across the sparkling water, its top hidden under a crown of clouds.

'Bananas!' Carlos said suddenly. 'You see?'

Laurie looked down as they flew over a banana plantation. This really was a magical island. For a moment, she thought of Jeremy sitting at the kitchen table behind his newspaper. Never in a million years would he do something like this. He would scoff and be scornful. She wondered how he'd respond if he did let himself go occasionally. Would something inside him loosen? And would he ever look up from his newspaper and see her for the woman she truly was? She had a feeling that it could never happen and that saddened her.

When had their love died? She really couldn't remember. It wasn't as if it was a particular date on the calendar.

March twenty-eighth 2020 – Jeremy stopped loving me and I started to resent him.

It had been a slow whittling away. A gradual fade. It made Laurie feel as if she'd failed somehow. A marriage was meant to be forever, wasn't it? But was that realistic when people were ever evolving? What if you and your chosen partner evolved in different directions? Is that what had happened to her and Jeremy? And what did that mean for their future together? *Together* being the word that gave her palpitations because she just couldn't imagine sharing the rest of her life with him.

But she didn't want to be thinking about all this now. Why was she giving him so much headspace in this glorious moment? Carlos was pointing something else out to her and she nodded as if she'd been listening.

They were fast approaching the coast and some very nice hotels. They'd dropped in height and she could clearly see people by a swimming pool reading novels and sipping drinks. How odd for them to be able to glance up and see people flying in the sky.

The ground was clearly visible now and she could see the people who had jumped before her. They'd landed on a sandy strip of land between the beach and the posh hotels, their colourful parachutes deflating after their moment of glory in the sky.

'What do I do with my legs?' Laurie yelled back to Carlos. He gave her some instructions but it all happened so fast, the ground rushing up to greet them, that Laurie wasn't at all sure she was in full command of her reaction. But, somehow, she remained upright and her feet made it onto terra firma.

She laughed. Her legs were shaking. Her whole body was shaking. She was breathless but so full of life.

Carlos laughed at her. 'You had a good time?'

'I loved it! I want to do it again!'

'Then I see you another time, Laurie!'

'Thank you!'

And then he was gone and a woman was approaching her with a clipboard and a credit card machine. It was time to buy the evidence.

After Laurie was dropped back at her hotel, she felt exhausted not just from the activity but because of the train of thought she'd had while dangling in mid-air. Her stomach was in knots because she'd admitted something to herself while up in the sky and it had broken her heart into a million pieces.

Her marriage was over. If she was totally honest, she'd known it for years but, what with little things like raising her children, holding down a full-time job and juggling all the demands of running a house, a trifling thing like a marriage falling apart hadn't taken centre stage in her brain.

But, here in Tenerife, after gifting herself time, she was able to focus and there was absolutely no denying that she'd reached a dead end as far as her relationship with Jeremy was concerned. There was nothing between them to even think about reigniting or resurrecting and that made her intensely sad. It was the slow death of a thousand little insults, ignored remarks and insensitive comments. Those were the silent assassins within a marriage. Or rather the *not so silent* assassins.

'I mustn't mope,' she told herself. 'I'm in paradise. Moping isn't allowed here.'

But it was going to take more than a quick reprimand to shake the melancholy off. Laurie knew she'd been living under melancholy's cloud for some time now, though there had been brief, teasing glimpses of hope. Somewhere beyond the horizon, she was certain, a better life was waiting for her. It felt as though she was living six miles south of happiness – close enough to know it existed, close enough to imagine she could see it if she tried hard enough. Yet it always remained just out of reach – that small, unbridgeable distance between her and the life she wanted.

Suddenly Laurie didn't want to be in her hotel room. She needed to get outside into the sunshine and gaze at the sea and the palm trees.

And she also needed to drown her sorrows with a drink and some junk food. She'd seen that there were no end of opportunities to eat poorly in Los Cristianos and she was going to make the most of it. First, she found a little place serving all-day English breakfasts – an absolute travesty on Spanish soil, but exactly what she wanted so she ordered one and washed it down with two cups of English tea. The dessert menu wasn't very inspiring though so she tried her luck elsewhere, walking down the long and lively row of seafront restaurants and cafés.

It wasn't long before she found exactly what she was looking for – a colourful little place selling smoothies and ice cream and everything in between that was colourful and calorific. Laurie placed her order and, a few minutes later, it arrived: an obscenely huge dessert served in a tall glass with a silver spoon, a pair of angel wing wafers and a little red umbrella poking out of its top. The multi-coloured layers of ice cream made Laurie feel instantly comforted and, when she ate the first spoonful, her worries simply left the building.

She wasn't going to think about cholesterol or dental cavities. She wouldn't dwell on diabetes or an expanding waistline. This was a moment of pure indulgence in which she was able to tune out all worries about the future. It was better than any yoga pose or breathing technique she'd learned the previous week and it beat the socks off any kind of meditation.

But, all too soon, she reached the bottom of the glass, her spoon scraping the last lovely gloopy drops. Would it be horribly greedy to order a second one? She glanced around at the other customers and felt as if everyone would notice and judge her so she reluctantly got up and left.

It wasn't much further down the seafront that she saw a woman sitting at a table eating her way through the biggest creamiest dessert Laurie had ever seen. Dare she?

She dared.

The second dessert was even more decadent than the first with ice cream, whipped cream and coloured sprinkles. It really was a work of art and Laurie couldn't resist taking a photo of it before she demolished it. Of course, she couldn't possibly order a third dessert, could she? Although it wouldn't be seen as her third – only her second, right? Still, even with her own skewed logic, Laurie did the decent thing and left. But her brain was now completely wired to look at each and every place she walked past, checking the colourful pictures on their menus and she simply couldn't resist the next place which looked so pretty with fairy lights and pink tables and chairs. She'd be sensible though. She wouldn't go overboard. She'd just have one small dessert.

By the time she got back to her hotel room, Laurie felt bloated and slightly nauseous. It served her right really. A grown woman doing that to herself was deplorable. And yet her full English breakfast and dessert crawl had felt so good in the moment. She'd make up for it tomorrow with an early morning swim and a fast-paced walk along the seafront. And she'd only eat healthy things for breakfast.

And no added sugar for the next week.

She shook her head. She'd never be able to keep to that.

And no added sugar for the next two days.

Or one day – at the very least!

CHAPTER FIFTEEN

After the disastrous phone call with Paul, Nuala recorded the video of her venting and uploaded it to YouTube without even watching it first. That, she thought, could be a huge mistake and could turn the small audience she'd built so far against her. Blow it! It was her channel, wasn't it? She'd never made any promises to her viewers as to what her content would be. But she knew she wanted to keep things real, and her argument with Paul was about as real as things got and she was jolly well going to share it. She was so angry and yet, at the same time, felt utterly invincible and there was, she hated to admit, a good proportion of her that was chanting, *This will teach him, this will teach him* as she watched the video uploading.

Then she'd gone to bed. It had been the strangest couple of days. First, she'd driven The Van onto a train and the pair of them had been whisked to France under the English Channel. Then she'd walked around Paris as if in a dream – those few perfect hours a prelude to the wobble she'd had when she'd felt convinced her adventure was over and it was time to go back to the UK and face whatever doom lay waiting for her. Then the phone call with Paul. Nuala didn't want to think about that again although, at the time, the anger it had induced had been a kind of fuel that was going to propel her forward on her journey into mainland Europe. And then the rant had happened. The filmed rant.

As she got up the next morning, holding her head in her hands because of the great thumping headache behind her temples, she couldn't help wondering if that was some kind of indication of the response she'd got. She was almost too nervous to look but, like ringing Paul, she knew she was going to have to face the consequences of her actions.

She put the kettle on and made a cup of tea, wishing she'd bought a couple more pastries from that shop in Paris to see her though this moment. She then switched her laptop on and waited for everything to load. She'd thought about getting a new one before the great European trip but had resisted because of all the other expenses they'd had. Now that she'd embraced life as a YouTuber, she was beginning to regret it. Perhaps she'd have to rethink that decision.

Once she'd finally logged on to YouTube, she visited a couple of her favourite channels first as she drank her tea, catching up on their new videos and leaving a friendly comment on both. It was nice to be a part of this new community. Even if she never met these women, it was still a kind of companionship that was most welcome on the road.

Then, when she could delay the moment no longer, she visited her own channel to see what damage she'd done. She really shouldn't have posted her video in the frame of mind she'd been in. It would probably be best if she quietly deleted it before anyone she knew saw it. Or, indeed, before *anyone* saw it!

But it was too late for that.

Nuala gasped as she saw the view count, thinking for a moment that she must be on the wrong page. But she wasn't. This was her page and it was definitely her video. As she stared at the thumbnail she'd chosen, she grimaced at her wild hair and the mad light in her eyes which made her look deranged.

'What was I thinking!' she whispered to herself.

She'd even forgotten about the title she'd chosen.

My Husband Told Me to Come Home. I took the RV to France Instead!

She looked at the view count again.

One hundred and fifty-eight thousand.

Some of her videos hadn't even been getting into the low hundreds so this figure was phenomenal. Maybe it was a blip. Maybe the platform was malfunctioning or something. She refreshed the page. The view count had gone up by another couple of hundred.

'This is insane!' Her mouth gaped in amazement.

But it wasn't just the view count that was insane – the comments section had gone crazy too. She had over eight hundred comments and people were even commenting on the comments. There were real-life conversations going on here. Until today, Nuala had been able to keep tabs on everything and had thought it good manners to reply to each and every comment – as long as it was polite, of course. She'd done a good job of that so far, but there'd be no way she could respond to everyone now.

She almost shut the laptop immediately because it was all so overwhelming but she really wanted to know what they were saying and so began to read.

Good for you, girl! You tell him!

He has every right to be mad at you. You need to sell the van quick!

Is that a hole in your jumper?

This woman's crazy! Should she even be driving?

She's not crazy – she's been lied to and cheated on!

You're my hero! Go on living your best life!

As she sat reading the comments, she was aware that her view count and subscriber number was going up all the time. It was quite mesmerising. She'd obviously hit a nerve even if a lot of people found her cringeworthy and crazy. And to think that she'd almost deleted the video.

She laughed. This was the very last thing she'd expected. She'd really had no preconceptions when she'd started her YouTube channel. Of course, she'd hoped to reach a viewership but she hadn't put a figure on it. She'd just wanted to document her personal journey, making something to look back on perhaps, and reach the sort of people who interested her and whose videos she was enjoying.

She watched as the views and subscribers continued to climb and began to recognise names in the comments such as RozinRome and CountryMouseUK who kindly left comments on all her videos. But there were hundreds – thousands – of others too. Who were all these people? She'd probably be able to see which countries and age groups they were in in the YouTube Studio somewhere. She hadn't really bothered with that yet and didn't want to get bogged down with the mechanics of this YouTube business.

The trouble was – would her new subscribers want more of the same? Would she have to remain the crazy, angry ex from now on? What if she wanted to make a video about tootling along the Loire Valley? Had she so quickly become a victim of the algorithm?

She read a few more of the comments and her thoughts were confirmed.

Tell us more about your scumbag husband!

We need more of this!

There isn't enough of this raw kind of honesty in the world anymore. Bring it on, Nuala!

It felt funny to see her name being used by total strangers. Her confession had opened a strange line of communication between her and the world and she could see, short of deleting everything and shutting her channel down, that there would be no stopping it.

But she could postpone it for now so she closed her laptop with a sigh of relief and focused on something that felt much more real: emptying The Van's toilet.

Elise was finally beginning to relax in Florence. She'd taken what she thought of as the 'heat' out of her trip by seeing all the big sites like the Duomo, The Uffizi and the Accademia. She'd crossed the Ponte Vecchio countless times and walked along the River Arno. She'd been completely floored by the Palazzo Vecchio – the 'Old Palace' with its ornate ceilings, fabulous map room and its views of the Duomo. She had spent a good couple of hours roaming its rooms and had adored the idea that she could spend even longer there if she so chose.

She'd followed in Lucy Honeychurch's footsteps to Santa Croce and had thoroughly indulged in her E M Forster dream of walking around the city like his young heroine although she felt a bit of a fraud aligning herself with that particular character now that she was in her fifties. And yet, at heart, Elise felt a kinship with the young woman who'd viewed Italy with the eyes of an innocent for, just like Lucy, Elise had seen so little of the world.

But you're seeing it now, she told herself.

She had eaten in some wonderful restaurants and had also shopped at markets for fresh produce and at supermarkets to keep her costs down, cooking at her new 'home'. And how she loved thinking of her tiny apartment as 'home'. It was incredible how very quickly you adapted, she couldn't help thinking. How a place you'd never known existed could soon become your home – your safe place, your hideaway from the world. With your clothes in the wardrobe, a couple of books on the bedside table and your food of choice in the fridge and cupboards, and toiletries in the bathroom, you could so quickly adapt and feel at peace.

She was even beginning to walk a little further off the tourist trail, discovering more local churches and streets – cafés and restaurants that the real residents of Florence patronised. But there was one place she'd been wanting to go into but hadn't quite got up the courage. She'd walked by several times but had lost her nerve at the last minute which was very silly really. It just looked so – well – nice. And that meant expensive. Elise hadn't quite got used to the fact that she actually had money in her bank account and that, if she so chose, she could buy herself some new clothes. Heaven only knew she deserved a few new pieces and she was all too aware that she wouldn't be in Florence forever. So, the next time she found herself walking past, she mustered up the courage and went inside.

The assistant behind the counter looked up and nodded

with a smile. She was serving a customer so that meant Elise could browse in peace for a while which was a real treat. She would have been much too shy to be in the spotlight of the assistant's attention. There was one other woman in the shop who was occupied trying on a jacket. She was well dressed with beautiful hair that swished and swirled over her shoulders most becomingly. Not like Elise's rebellious curls. Self-consciously, Elise flattened her hair down and wished, not for the first time, that she had fine, straight hair that behaved itself.

It was a strange experience to be in such a beautiful boutique shop. Elise had never been fashion-led and got most of her pieces online from well-known companies that were a little old-fashioned, perhaps. Safe and predictable. Nothing too daring. She caught sight of herself in the mirror now and grimaced at the navy jumper she was wearing over a pair of very dull beige trousers. Now a navy jumper and beige trousers can be the very height of elegance but not the combination Elise had on, alas. They were horrible, dull and dated and did her pretty figure no justice. The jumper was too dark on her and much too baggy and the trousers were too short and boxy. It wasn't a look she loved. What she was really after was more Grace Kelly from the 1950s – elegant and feminine . In short, she could benefit from a makeover, but she didn't know where to begin.

Colour perhaps. She could introduce a bit of colour into her life. She'd once had her colours analysed professionally. It had been something that had fascinated her for years and she'd treated herself to an afternoon assessment with a woman called Cherry who'd informed her that she was an 'Autumn'. Elise liked that. The rich, warm colours, the dusky muted shades suited her

personality. She still had the colour swatches somewhere. She must dig them out some time and try to get things right.

In the meantime, a dusky pink top caught her eye and she reached out to feel the fabric at the precise moment that a woman next to her did the same thing. Their hands touched and Elise leapt back in surprise.

'Scusi!" she cried.

'I'm so sorry!' the woman said at the same time.

Elise looked her. It was the woman who'd been trying on the jacket at the back of the shop. 'You're English?'

'Yes! You?'

'Yes.'

They exchanged smiles.

'Do you live here?' the woman asked.

'Yes,' Elise said automatically. 'That is, for a little while. Not permanently. At least – well... I'm not sure. I have a home back in the UK, but haven't decided if I want to stay there.'

'Sounds... interesting!' the woman said.

Elise laughed. 'I'm still working things out.'

'That's nice.'

'How about you?' Elise asked. 'On holiday?'

'Yes and an all too brief one.'

'Travelling solo?'

'No, I'm here with my husband.'

Elise looked around the shop.

'Oh, he's not here.' The woman inched a little closer. 'We're having some alone time,' she whispered and then giggled. 'Vital to a long marriage. He's gone to see some gallery which would bore me silly and I'm indulging in a bit of shopping which would bore him silly. So, tonight, when

we meet up, we'll both be happy and fulfilled and absolutely delighted to see one another again having had a good break.'

Elise smiled. 'I love that.'

'It's healthy, right? I mean, we're not joined at the hip, are we? We don't have to see everything together *all* the time.'

'No, I think that's a great idea.'

'It shocks some people,' the woman confessed. 'One of my friends thinks it's practically sinful. But I really don't see the sense in us being bored rigid by each other's passions, do you?' She laughed. 'Listen, I'm babbling on here. Let me leave you to shop in peace.' She motioned back to the item they'd both been about to grab.

'It's okay – I was just looking,' Elise said. 'It's actually fun to talk in English with someone. I'm not sure I've spoken more than a dozen English words since I got to Italy.'

'You're fluent in Italian?'

'I wouldn't say that. But I do try and make an effort.'

'It's a beautiful language. I should make more of an effort myself but you know how that goes and it seems like a lot of work for just one holiday a year. Especially with Google Translate now. I just talk into that and present it to anyone who doesn't speak English. Is that awful of me?'

'No!' Elise assured her. 'It's just being practical.'

'Listen – this might sound forward, but do you fancy getting coffee or a bite to eat? My feet are killing me. I've just bought these shoes and they're not proving good companions for a lot of walking.'

'Oh dear.' Elise glanced down at the pretty but impractical heeled shoes her new friend was wearing. They were poppy red and really rather stunning, but Elise was glad she'd got her sensible white pumps on for getting around the cobbles of Florence.

'I'm Andie, by the way.'

'Elise.'

They shook hands and then laughed at the very English formality.

'I know the perfect place,' Elise told her, leading the way out of the shop. She allowed herself a private little smile as she told Andie about an area of Florence that was very dear to her. It felt like a very grown-up thing to be showing a new friend to a café in Florence. Elise knew that it was an odd thought to have but she'd never really felt like a grown-up. Perhaps it was the years of being under the control of her mother. She'd always been a daughter, hadn't she? She'd never been allowed to be an adult in her own right. As long as her mother had been alive, Elise had been a child to be bossed about and ruled over. But not anymore. Here in Florence, she was slowly coming into herself. She was being born again – having her own Florentine renaissance. She smiled at the thought of that. It could almost be the title of a novel by E M Forster's Eleanor Lavish: *The Renaissance of Elise Cherrington*.

Passing the Palazzo Pitti and turning down a side street lined with pretty shops, Elise continued to lead the way until they came to the small café. Opening the door, she inhaled the sweet scent of coffee that she knew she would carry with her forever. The owner glanced up from the counter with a friendly smile.

'Buongiorno! Come stai? Sei tornato per un altro caffè, vero?'

'Ma certo. È il migliore di Firenze, Bruno!' Elise replied, ordering two coffees and a couple of pastries before taking their seats by a window overlooking the street.

'Listen to you! You're practically a local now!' Andie told her.

Elise laughed. 'I was just telling him that his coffee is the best in Florence.'

'I really should try to learn some Italian. It sounds so beautiful. When did you learn?'

'Oh, years ago. I'd always wanted to come to Italy. I had this dream to study here, live here amongst all the beauty. Not very original, I know, but I couldn't make it work over the years.'

'Still you're here now.'

'Yes,' Elise said. 'I'm here now.'

'That's all that matters really, isn't it?' Andie said. 'The "now". That's what I'm learning anyway,' she added. 'I went to this retreat last year. Ed wanted to go on a hiking holiday and I really didn't fancy that so I booked a spiritual retreat and it was all about learning to live in the present moment. You'd be surprised how hard that is sometimes.'

'Oh, no. I totally get how difficult it is,' Elise said, thinking of how her own nightmare about her mother had so quickly dragged her back into the past.

'It gave me a real appreciation of the passing of time,' Andie shared. 'And maybe that's made me a little selfish when it comes to holidays and days like today because I don't want to waste a single minute doing something I don't want to do.'

'Then I'm very honoured you're here with me now,' Elise acknowledged as their coffees and pastries arrived at the table.

'Are you kidding? This place is heavenly! If you'd taken me to some dive, I'd have been out of here in a hot minute!'

Elise smiled. 'How's your pastry?'

Andie took her first mouthful and then giggled and covered her face with her paper napkin. 'Oh, my god! It's to *die* for!'

Elise nodded knowingly. She'd become somewhat addicted to Bruno's pastries.

'But everything in Italy's to die for, isn't it? The food, the wine, the architecture, the men! But especially the food. It's a good job I don't live here. I'd bloat and explode in no time. Just as well we live in the UK where the bread and pastries are so dire that I don't even bother.'

Elise laughed. She hadn't thought of that before, but it was kind of true. Every time she'd ever treated herself to a baguette at home, it was sorely disappointing especially anything from a supermarket. They were too big and baggy with no flavour whatsoever. And the pastries just weren't the same either. But here was a different matter altogether. It was virtually impossible to walk passed a *pasticceria* without popping in to buy something wickedly divine.

'Goodness only knows what will happen to my waistline,' Elise said. 'I'm in Italy for the next couple of months at least.'

Andie shook her head as she took a sip of her coffee. 'There's no hope for you then. You're well and truly sunk!'

'I think you might be right.'

'Still – it's a nice way to go.'

They laughed again.

'So tell me what brought you to Florence,' Andie said.

Elise took a sip of her coffee. How much detail did she want to go into? How much would be polite to reveal on a first meeting with someone?

'Well, my mother died recently,' she began, deciding to jump right in.

'Oh, I'm so sorry. Were you close?'

'Not exactly. I mean, I saw her every day but...' she paused. 'It was complicated.'

Andie reached across the table and squeezed her hand. 'You don't have to go into details if you don't want to, darling.'

Elise swallowed hard, surprised by both her new friend's gesture and the kindness of her voice.

'Anyway, she left me some money and, let's just put it this way, I was never able to get away while she was alive.'

Andie nodded. 'I see.'

'And I've longed to return to Italy. I had a false start a long time ago and have been dreaming of getting back ever since. How about you? What brought you here?'

'Oh, the usual – beautiful things to see and fabulous food. I think us Brits have a love affair with this country, don't we? And we don't quite feel complete until we've got it out of our system. Ed and I honeymooned on the Amalfi coast and we've been coming back ever since. This is our fourth trip to Florence.'

'It's funny how some places get hold of you,' Elise said, wondering if she'd be lucky enough to come back to Florence a third and a fourth time.'

'And you're here on your own?' Andie asked.

'Yes!'

'That's very brave of you. I'm not sure I could do that.'

Elise smiled. 'It doesn't feel very brave – just necessary. I mean, I'm a fifty-something single woman. I don't have any family – at least not any close by who'd want to come with me. My few friends all have partners or dependants. I don't like the idea of group tours. So that just leaves me.' She shrugged. 'I told somebody at work I was going away on my own and she looked at me as though I was crazy. But I think it would be crazier of me not to come. It's either me doing this on my own or not at all. That's how I see it. And, yes, it's scary. I get a little nervous every time I leave my apartment here, and I'm already getting anxious about moving on to the next place. When I think of all the things that could go wrong like having an accident or a medical emergency or getting on the wrong train. And I'm absolutely terrified of losing or breaking my phone or getting something stolen and – well – you get the idea. But then I remember that all those things could just as easily happen to me at home. I could fall down the stairs in my own house or have a stroke in bed or get knocked over by a bus in my home town. So isn't it sensible – sane even – to not let fear stop you?'

'I'd never thought of it like that,' Andie said. 'But you're right. Staying at home is just as risky as venturing out into the world.'

'I think it's actually worse because it keeps you small. And I should know.'

Andie looked at her with a sweetness Elise hadn't seen in anyone's eyes in such a long time.

'So I'm not brave. Not really. I'm scared *all* the time, I really am! But I'm also excited and grateful and very determined.'

'Well, I think you're marvellous. Really! It's so inspiring. Maybe I'll book more solo trips in the future.'

'You should!'

It was then that Andie's phone beeped and she took it out of her bag.

'Oh, dear! It's Ed. He's done at the museum and wants to know if I'm still shopping.' She glanced up at Elise. 'Am I still shopping?'

Elise paused and then grinned. 'Yes. I think you still are.'

The two women laughed and ordered more coffee and pastries.

By the time Elise got back to her apartment, she was happily exhausted. It had been so much fun meeting Andie. She hadn't talked and laughed like that in years and she'd forgotten how good it felt. It had been sad to say goodbye. They'd exchanged numbers but Andie and her husband were heading south to Sorrento soon and Elise didn't think they'd meet up again. Still, swapping numbers was what you did, wasn't it? Elise was out of touch with making friends in the real world. Her world had been so small for years. But maybe this was the way with making friends while travelling. You just connected briefly. You were friends for a few hours. Sometimes, that's all that was needed. It would be wrong to try and turn it into something that it wasn't. They had found each other at precisely the moment they both needed and that was enough.

CHAPTER SIXTEEN

Laurie had had a full day – she'd taken a day trip up to Mount Teide, riding the cable car to the summit and walking the rocky path at the top where the world was so silent it had taken her breath away. She'd visited the national park on an excursion when at her yoga retreat but hadn't had the chance to actually venture up the volcano itself. The air was slightly sulphurous, but she had loved every minute. The red rawness of the landscape had made her feel that she was on another planet entirely, but this was Earth at its barest and most brilliant. The size of the landscape had put her very much in her place, making her feel absolutely tiny. Of course, you can't visit a volcano without mulling over your own mortality. She wasn't sure about Teide's record, but she knew it was an active volcano and there'd been rumours on the coach going up that it was definitely due to blow. Didn't everyone say that about volcanoes though? It certainly added an element of drama to the excursion.

As she'd sat on a rock close to the summit, she hadn't been able to help contemplating how she'd feel if the end were to come while she was there. Would she be peaceful or panicking? Would she be grateful for the life she'd had or regretful that she hadn't lived enough? Would she be content? She hadn't been able to answer those questions to her true satisfaction. She knew she wanted to live more – *truly* live. Her brief time away from her home, job and family had so far shown her that there was more of her to discover and she was beginning to like what – or rather *who* – she was becoming.

By the time the coach had done all the coastal drop-offs and pulled up outside Laurie's hotel, she'd been too tired to think of heading into town so had taken a shower and a nap in her room. It felt very naughty doing that in what was essentially the middle of the day. She'd still have at least two hours of work ahead of her if she'd been at the office. Oh, how that life seemed eons ago now and what a blessed relief. And how very thoroughly she'd embraced this new life of getting up each morning and venturing out into the world to see new things. This way of living was so incredibly revolutionary to her – that the world was here to be enjoyed and that she was here to do that very enjoying. She hadn't been forged and created to work all the hours God sent. When exactly had humans put themselves in such ghastly cages? What a waste of this one beautiful life – to lock ourselves away in jobs that were very often detested. She only hoped that she had woken up early enough during the span of her life to truly make the most of every single moment from now on.

After getting up from her nap, Laurie spent a bit of time catching up with everyone. She'd been messaging Jeremy to let him know she was okay, but the brief texts she'd had back didn't encourage her to try any harder. One of them had simply read:

Where did you put the teabags?

Laurie hadn't responded to that one.

She'd only had one reply from her son who'd told her to 'Have fun!' She saw that as a clear end to that line of communication. Her daughter was a little more interested in what she was up to.

Send me a pic! Tilly had said on more than one occasion which was quite heartening.

But it was Kitty whom she'd kept in touch with the most. Since saying their goodbyes at the airport after the yoga retreat, they'd swapped messages every day on WhatsApp and had sent each other photos of what they'd been up to. The ones Kitty had sent from Seville were very inspiring. Laurie definitely had that city very firmly on her list of must-see places.

Putting her phone down, she walked out onto her balcony. It was an ugly grey concrete thing, but it did allow her to test the temperature and she knew it was too nice to stay indoors a moment longer. That was the joy of a subtropical climate – you could enjoy the outdoor life well into the evening so she grabbed a light jumper and headed into town.

When you were a solo female traveller, shopping was a rite of passage, although it could make life a little tricky if you were trying to travel light. Laurie had promised herself an indulgent shopping trip – not indulgent in that she was intending to buy lots of things, but because she would allow herself the time to simply drift from shop to shop looking at and trying on whatever caught her eye.

The shops in Los Cristianos were full of the sort of thing

that could very quickly take you over the Ryanair cabin allowance. Alcohol, cigarettes, gaudy plastic souvenirs and more cheap clothes than Laurie had ever seen. It was brilliant. This was just the sort of place Jeremy despised and would never be seen dead shopping in, but Laurie filled her sense with the colours and shapes of absolutely everything. It was fun to simply wander the backstreets especially in the evening as the sun was setting and the dark silhouettes of the palm trees were swaying in the breeze from the sea. It was still warm and there were plenty of people around shopping like her or sitting outside restaurants. Laurie was tempted to get something to eat but she knew she should probably give her system a rest as she'd been eating so much junk food since leaving the yoga retreat and that didn't really align with her vow to take care of herself: *body* and soul.

She was just walking past a restaurant where the waft of curry on the warm night air nearly stopped her in her tracks when she saw the dress in a shop window opposite. Ignoring the scent of food, she crossed the crowded street and gazed into the window.

The dress wasn't like anything Laurie had in her wardrobe at home. It was short, bright and cheap. It was also very green – chartreuse, perhaps. The green of spring light filtered through new beech tree leaves. Vivid and alive. And that was enough to get Laurie into the shop.

A young assistant looked up from where she was stacking cheap sunglasses on a mirrored shelf.

'Hola!' Laurie said.

The assistant smiled and said something in Spanish which Laurie didn't understand and so she smiled back and nodded as if she had comprehended perfectly.

She motioned to the dress in the window and the

assistant pointed to a section at the back of the shop where a few were hanging up. Laurie pulled one out, wondering what size she was. It was so long since she'd bought herself a new dress that she really didn't know.

Taking it into the dressing room at the back of the shop, she immediately regretted her choice as soon as she attempted to pull it down over her body. It was far too small and the zip at the side gaped wide and unforgivingly, mocking her for her innumerable desserts of late. The days of 'small' were long over, she lamented. What with having what she termed her "mum belly" and the comfort eating she'd succumbed to during menopause, she really should have brought in two sizes to try on. Now, she'd have to sneak out of the changing room with the small dress gaping open and hope that the assistant wouldn't see.

She drew back the curtain as quietly as possible and tiptoed across the shop. Of course, the assistant looked up immediately and said something. Laurie hesitated mid-step. What was "too small" in Spanish? She had no idea. So she pointed to the rail and the assistant, glancing at the gaping dress, nodded in comprehension and retrieved another from the rail.

'*Gracias!*' Laurie managed, slinking back to the changing room, lesson learned.

Ah, yes, this was the one, she thought as she pulled the dress over her head and it cascaded down her body with ease. There was no protest from the zip either. Instead, it glided up and cinched her in beautifully. She attempted to bend forward and did a little squat. Such things were important to be able to do. The dress acquiesced. She felt around her tummy to see if there was any give – just in case she wanted to indulge. There was give. It even had two discreet pockets.

Could she have found the perfect dress?

Whether or not she had, she loved it! She ran her hands down the bright fabric which gently kissed her knees. Who would have thought her legs would look this good in a dress like this? She tried to imagine Jeremy's reaction to it but really didn't want to. He'd be appalled and tell her to put one of her old ankle-skimming dresses on – one in a heavy, mumsy print that covered absolutely everything up and left no room for the sun to find her.

To be honest, she wasn't sure what had happened to her style over the years. She'd used to love choosing a few new fashionable pieces for her wardrobe each season. When had that stopped, she wondered? When she'd become pregnant? Had she lost interest in her own body after that and focused her attention – and wallet – on her little ones? She thought about her wardrobe now and the dowdy clothes in muted colours that did neither her colouring nor her confidence any good at all.

Seeing herself in this dress now, Laurie had a glimpse not only of the woman she had once been but of the woman she could become. This, she thought, was the kind of dress a woman could have an adventure in.

She would wear it on her trip to the island of La Gomera tomorrow.

Elise had been in Florence for a full three weeks before she took her Great Aunt Clara's sketchbook into the city with her. Although she'd used it initially as inspiration and encouragement to take her trip around Europe, she hadn't wanted it to be her crutch. She'd been determined to find her way around Florence first and make the city her own. Seeing it through her eyes had been very important. But she now felt ready to take the sketchbook out with her and try to find where some of the beautiful paintings and sketches had been done.

One of the watercolours was a detail from a statue in the Loggia della Signoria. The fourteenth-century loggia was a favourite sight of hers in the city. Standing adjacent to the Palazzo Vecchio, the loggia was a kind of exhibition space – open fronted with three large arches and shallow steps leading into the vaulted space full of impressive statues. Elise had visited the loggia several times on this trip and had taken many photographs of it. It had played a key role in a scene in the film adaptation *A Room with a View* and was a popular place for tourists to congregate. It had even been the inspiration for E M Forster's lady novelist's book – *Under a Loggia*.

Clara had written *Athena under Perseus, Loggia della Signoria* in neat sloping script.

Elise knew the statue well. It was hard to miss. The bronze by Benvenuto Cellini dated from the mid-sixteenth century and was a real crowd pleaser. But it hadn't been the statue Clara had sketched – rather a detail from the ornate plinth it was on. Elise wondered why she hadn't sketched Perseus himself holding the head of the Medusa. It was the famous part of the statue after all, but maybe it was a little too obvious. It seemed that Clara had enjoyed zoning in on the details. It was also quite gruesome. Who'd want to look at something so gory for an extended time – however impressive it was?

So, instead of the main attraction, Clara had sketched the beautiful head and upper torso of the goddess Athena who appeared several times around the plinth. Surrounded by spiralling acanthus leaves, she was quite a sight to behold and certainly a little less startling than the slain Medusa.

Elise had to admit that she hadn't paid any attention to the plinth before because it was Perseus and Medusa who stole the attention – the size and the drama of the piece were all-consuming. Glancing around, she saw that nobody else was looking at lovely Athena either. The Greek goddess, who had helped Perseus in his mission to slay Medusa, was very firmly relegated here. A side note to the famous story. A bit player. Elise wondered what Athena would make of that.

She loved that Clara had chosen to sketch the lovely feminine features of Athena rather than the overtly masculine energy of Perseus and she couldn't help wondering where she'd stood while she was sketching – or perhaps she'd sat. Would she have brought a foldable chair with her? Elise wished she could travel back in time and witness the moment.

The other thing Elise had been wondering was if they might have become friends if they'd crossed paths. It seemed as if they were drawn to the same places and things, but that was no guarantee that you'd get on with somebody. If Elise had been walking across the piazza and seen a woman sketching, would she have approached her? Might a conversation have started and developed? Would they have spent time together as she and Andie had done? There were so many tantalising questions about the past that would forever remain unanswered. But it was fun to imagine. Great Aunt Clara was beginning to become ever more important to Elise on her journey and very much felt like a friend.

It was a joy to spend time in the Piazza della Signoria even if you had to jostle with the throng of tourists. Elise had to remind herself that, even if she was slow travelling and practically living in the city, she was still a tourist and doing exactly the same thing as everyone else. There was a tendency, she'd read, for slow travellers to place themselves above other tourists. Even the words used on the social media sites had connotations. The notion that a "traveller" was somehow different from and more special – maybe even more sensitive – than a mere 'tourist'. Elise thought it was all just snobbery. Some people would always feel the need to place themselves a couple of rungs higher than other people, but Elise had no such pretentions. She was just happy to be here.

Her job at Bevington House had made her all too aware of the importance of travel in the past and how the aristocracy in particular had enjoyed the privilege of not only seeing the beauty of foreign cities such as Florence but of carrying or sending half of it back to install in their own homes. The Grand Tour had been a rite of passage between the seventeenth and nineteenth centuries when the wealthy upper classes would complete their education by experiencing the cultural wonders that places like Florence offered. Indeed Bevington House had many pieces from Italy which had come from generations of the family spending small fortunes on artworks and furniture, including a very fine Canaletto painting of Venice which, rather miraculously, had survived many rounds of death duties over the years. The current owners were always threatening to sell it so they could do some dull job like repair the roof or install new plumbing, but it would be too heart-wrenching to lose such a beautiful object.

Elise's purchases were far more modest by comparison. She might have treated herself to a few new clothes and a beautiful handmade notebook, but she certainly wasn't looking to buy expensive art. The camera on her phone would have to capture the magic instead. Besides she already possessed the loveliest art in the form of Great Aunt Clara's sketchbook.

She turned the page now to the next Florentine image. This was a pretty watercolour of a fresco with the name of the church it appeared in. Elise looked it up on Google Maps and started in what she hoped was the right direction, taking in a few other sites as she went.

It was only after a full hour of walking that it dawned on her that she might have taken a wrong turn somewhere as she seemed to have ended up in a more modern part of Florence. The glories of the Renaissance had been replaced with bigger, brasher buildings. She tried not to panic, but Google Maps didn't seem to be helping no matter which way she turned her phone. She tried resetting her position, but really couldn't make head nor tail of it. She was getting hungry too now and she needed the loo.

She quickly took in her surroundings. It was always a bit of an issue when you were out all day as to where you'd find a nice clean toilet. It was okay if you were planning a sit down meal and could use the facilities there, but Elise would often want to spend her time exploring and eat back at her apartment in the evening once it was dark so as not to lose a single minute discovering more of Florence. She had, on occasion, nipped into a nice hotel lobby and found ground floor toilets. The posher the hotel, the easier it seemed to be as people were coming and going all the time and there were often cafés, restaurants and even shops in the better hotels. She'd also done the same with large cafés with outdoor seating. You just had to look confident when walking inside.

But this area seemed devoid of all opportunities for a needy tourist and she was beginning to get anxious.

It was then that she noticed a modern building overlooking a small park. There were rather a lot of people coming and going and she watched for a moment. Some were carrying briefcases and they all seemed to be wearing lanyards. It seemed to be some sort of conference. There were banners waving outside and a definite buzz in the air. She'd take her chance there.

Approaching the glass doors, Elise hoped she could just walk casually inside without being stopped by security. As she entered the building, she noticed a reception desk. Luckily, there was a group of people already there which gave Elise a chance to look at the floor plan by the stairwell. Toilets: first and third floors. She took the stairs, following a woman in a crisp navy suit. Elise looked down at her own attire: the pink dress she was wearing did make her stand out somewhat. She'd just have to look extra confident.

The first floor opened out and Elise saw little stalls with tables had been set up all around the room. It was busy and noisy and she was able to slip through everybody unnoticed and find the toilets. She smiled wryly to herself as she locked herself in a cubicle and couldn't help feeling a little bit naughty, but she was quite sure she wasn't the only traveller – or rather tourist – to make the most of any given opportunity.

After washing her hands, giving her hair a quick brush and readjusting her hat, she headed back onto the conference floor and spotted an escalator. It would be quicker than the stairs to make her exit. She felt very lucky indeed that she wasn't spending all day cooped up in a conference centre in a modern part of town wearing navy. She was able to drift back outside to the beauty of the old Florence in her pink dress and hat.

She was just about to step onto the escalator when a man caught her eye. For a moment, she thought he was about to challenge her and she'd have the terrible embarrassment of explaining what she'd been doing, but he merely smiled and gestured that she should go first.

'*Grazie!*'

'*Prego,*' he responded.

It was a relief to get back outside and she quickly found a little corner shop and bought a sandwich, taking it to the park she'd seen. Most of the benches were full of people in suits, their lanyards catching the light. Elise found the last vacant one and sat down, but she was soon joined by a man who asked if he could sit next to her. She looked up to give a nod and saw that it was the man from the top of the escalator.

'*Grazie,*' he said.

'*Prego,*' she responded and they grinned at one another.

'You're English?' he asked.

'Yes. How could you tell? Was it my accent or my hat?'

'Both. It's a very nice hat. And accent.' He laughed. He had a nice laugh.

She watched as he opened a boxed sandwich and began to eat. 'The food in there's not great,' he explained. 'I think they've skimped on the caterers this year, no?'

'Oh, I'm not...' she paused and his eyebrows rose. 'I'm not attending.'

'Day visit?'

'No.' Oh, dear, Elise thought. It was confession time. She'd just *known* she'd be found out.

'I was just...'

'What?'

'I came in to use the facilities.'

He frowned and then realisation dawned. 'Ah, I see!'

Elise could feel herself blushing. 'They were very good.'

'I thought – well – you looked different. Your dress. And hat.'

'I'm afraid I rather stood out in there, didn't I?'

'But in a good way.' He smiled again.

Was he flirting with her? It felt like an age since somebody had done that. It was a nice feeling and he was quite handsome in a buttoned-down sort of way with his crisp sky-blue shirt and navy jacket and trousers. He had neat-cropped hair and deep brown eyes which had a mischievous glint in their dark depths.

'I'm Paolo,' he said. 'From Milano.'

'Paolo from Milano!' she repeated.

'I love the way that sounds with your accent,' he said.

She did her best not to blush again, but it wasn't entirely within her control. 'I'm Elise from – well, you probably wouldn't have heard of it. A small town in the Midlands.'

'You're right. I know only of London... and Oxford.'

'And do you like them?'

'Oxford I liked, yes. Beautiful! London was too chaotic. I didn't like the trains – the underground.'

'The Tube?'

'Yes! Too many lines. Too many people.'

'But you live in Milan.'

'Yes. But there are only five metro lines there. Nice and easy.'

She smiled. 'I will remember that if I visit.'

'You're visiting Milano?'

'I don't know yet. Maybe. I'd love to see the duomo.'

'You must! And let me know when you're there. I'll take you to my favourite places, *si?*'

Elise looked at him. He looked sincere enough and it would be nice to have a contact in a big city like Milan to show her around.

'Okay,' she said, feeling a little wary but excited too.

'Great!' They exchanged numbers on their phones.

'So what's the conference about?' she asked.

'Ah, much too dull to talk about when the sun is shining.'

'But I'm interested,' she insisted.

'It's very boring – really. Computer stuff. AI stuff. *Stuffy stuff!*'

She smiled.

'Tell me what you're doing in Firenze. That's much more *interessante!*'

'Well, I'm here to see... everything!'

'Everything?'

'*Il tutto* – is that right?'

'*Sì!*'

'I've got a little apartment for a month so I can really explore the city,' she told him and then caught herself. Perhaps it wasn't a good idea to tell a strange man that she was staying in an apartment by herself for a whole month. 'My friend Andie, is with me,' she added quickly. Well, Andie had been with her – only very briefly.

Paolo nodded. 'And what do you think of *Firenze?*'

'*Bellissima!*'

'And what have you seen?'

Elise told him about the galleries and museums, the churches and the shops and the little corners she'd been exploring in search of her great aunt's sketches. She even showed him the one she was pursuing now. Maybe she was getting too familiar with him too quickly, but it felt natural. Wasn't that one of the joys of travelling – to meet new people? It would be a bit sad if you returned home having only seen a few beautiful buildings.

'Listen,' Paolo said, leaning forward ever so slightly. 'I know of the most beautiful piazza near here. I bet you haven't seen it yet. Not many tourists find their way there. I think you'll appreciate it. You have...' he paused, 'the gift of seeing, I think, *si?*'

She smiled, feeling flattered by his praise.

'I'll take you there – *subito!*'

'But the conference? Don't you have to—'

'Pah! That can wait!' He shook his hands in a dismissive manner making Elise laugh. '*È una bella giornata.* It's a beautiful day.' He gestured to the sky.

All the warnings were there – going off with a man she'd only just met. But they'd be in public, wouldn't they? She looked at him, aware of the sparkle in his brown eyes.

'Let me show you this special place, Elise,' he said, seeing her hesitation.

'I...,' she paused. She was definitely teetering, weighing up the pros and cons, the pluses and minuses, the wonders and the worries.

It was then that a woman walked towards them. Her steps were fast and her expression was furious.

'Paolo!' she cried. Her voice might have been addressing him, but her stony grey eyes were fixed on Elise.

'Ah!' Paolo said, slapping his hands on his legs. Elise stared at him, waiting for an explanation, but he only gave her a funny little smile.

'Time to get back,' he said with a little shrug.

'Yes,' Elise said. 'It would seem that way, wouldn't it?'

Paolo got up from the bench and Elise watched as the woman practically marched him back to the conference centre and she couldn't help thinking that it probably wasn't the first time she'd had to do that.

She finished her sandwich, laughing at the scenario and reprimanding herself for having very nearly been swept up by his charm. Quickly, she got out her phone and deleted and blocked his number.

She never did find the little church with the fresco which Aunt Clara had painted. But that was okay. She'd had a different kind of adventure that day, hadn't she?

CHAPTER SEVENTEEN

After leaving the campsite outside Paris, Nuala headed south-west towards the Loire Valley. She was so looking forward to seeing it and it should look glorious in the spring, she thought. Famous for its many fairytale chateaux, its rolling countryside and pretty towns dotted along the river, she was going to enjoy exploring. She had a big, long list of all the chateaux she wanted to see: Chateau de Chambord was the largest and looked an impressive sight with its fat round turreted towers; Chateau de Villandry was famous for its wonderful Renaissance gardens; and Chateau d'Azay-le-Rideau was built on an island which apparently made it look like it was floating.

But the one she was most looking forward to was Chateau de Chenonceau. Online photos showed its white gloriousness straddling a river, its elegant arches making the most wonderful reflections. There was something about the sturdiness of the building mirrored in the delicacy of the water that appealed to Nuala. She'd never really been in to castles in the UK. Paul had always enjoyed poking around old English castles from the ruins of Bolton Castle in the Yorkshire Dales – where poor Mary Queen of Scots was held prisoner within its cold, damp walls – to the sprawling splendour of Warwick Castle, which had freaked Nuala out with its waxwork figures.

The French chateaux, however, fired something up inside her. Perhaps it was just the picture book perfection of them which appealed to the little girl who was still hiding somewhere inside every woman: the girl who had grown up reading Ladybird fairytale books and watching Disney princesses. Her mother had a lot to answer for putting those images into her head at an impressionable age. Still, what was life without a little bit of fantasy – even if Nuala had had to wake up to the fact that her prince had definitely turned into a frog.

As she drove south, Nuala determined not to give the frog in her life any more headspace. She was heading somewhere very special indeed: the magnificent Chateau de Chambord. She was a little anxious that, by starting with the biggest, the others might disappoint, but she thought they each had a charm of their own and that biggest didn't always mean best. Still, when she got her first glimpse of the enormous building rising high above the flat landscape that sprawled around it, she really couldn't imagine another chateau topping it.

Begun in 1519 as a royal hunting lodge, it was a veritable city in stone. Barrel-vaulted ceilings embossed with salamander carvings and gold-framed hunting scenes and enormous tapestries on the walls vied for attention and Nuala drifted along the blond stone corridors into spacious rooms, taking her time, glorying in the gorgeousness of it all.

A spiral staircase led up to the rooftop terrace where

Nuala walked amongst the spires, chimneys and turrets and stood absolutely still to admire the expanse of garden, grounds and woods which seemed to stretch for miles. It felt good to be still, to be able to rest her eyes without the strain of driving. She felt as if she'd been in motion ever since she'd left her marital home behind.

She bought a very expensive tin of biscuits from the gift shop. It was silly really. She'd get much better value from a supermarché or even a boulangerie. But she liked the image of the chateau on it and thought it would be a nice souvenir to keep things in for The Van. She did, of course, see the danger of starting to collect things having only just purged herself of a lifetime of possessions. How easy it would be to fill The Van to bursting point. She mustn't let things get out of hand again. Buying stuff was a very slippery slope.

As she returned to the car park, she realised just how much time she'd spent at the chateau. There was definitely no way she would be able to see another today. She was truly chateauxed out. Luckily, though, she could save the others for future days – going at her own pace leisurely and lovingly. She could only imagine Paul's horror at the itinerary she had in mind. He might put up with visiting one or two but he'd seriously draw the line at any more than that. Well, that was one of the joys of it just being her now. She could indulge every little romantic whim that she had.

But, alas, her grand tour of the fairytale settings of France wasn't meant to be. Having enjoyed a happy hour plotting her route to enable her to see as many chateaux and pretty towns as possible, Nuala was completely unaware that The Van had other plans.

There had been the briefest of warnings after she'd left

the outskirts of Paris: a faint crackling, a little blinking of screens and a soft clicking behind the dashboard. It was just technology having a moment, Nuala told herself. There was nothing to worry about. The Van was still moving. However, when there was a slight hesitation as she started to accelerate up a hill shortly after leaving Chateau de Chambord, she began to have misgivings. The steering wheel felt a little stiffer than normal and she was quite sure there was a hot plastic – or even metallic – smell coming from the dashboard vents.

It was just as she was passing through the sort of quaint little French village that would absolutely merit stopping that The Van decided she was, indeed, going to stop there – for quite some time. The dashboard lights began to flicker as if possessed and the radio cut out right in the middle of Nuala's favourite part of a song which she took as a very bad omen indeed. A sharp pop followed by silence as the engine cut out was the death knell.

Suddenly Nuala's anxious breaths were the loudest thing in The Van along with the ticking of cooling metal. Somehow she managed to coast into a passing place just outside the village and felt grateful that she hadn't progressed any further away from civilisation.

But The Van was brand new. Should it be having issues so soon? Well, whether or not it should be having issues, it seemed that it *was* having them. Had Nuala inadvertently done something she shouldn't have that had caused it to break down? She took her seat belt off and stared at the dashboard in disbelief. For a moment she panicked, wondering what would happen if The Van needed a lot of work doing to it and if she could go on living in it while it was being repaired. She didn't like the idea of cooking or showering inside if there was somebody actually working on it. But this was an issue. The Van wasn't just her transport, it was her accommodation and an important part of the trip she'd budgeted for. Heaven only knew she'd paid enough for it but to have to shell out now for somewhere to stay as well as the repairs – that really was the limit.

Still, there was no use railing against the facts. She was in a fix and she had to pay to get herself out of it. At least she hadn't been in an accident. The problem was probably fixable and she would be on her way again soon, she hoped. She was fast learning that travel was a bit like buying a bargain lot at auction – it wasn't just a collection of fabulous experiences, it was also traffic jams and getting lost and breaking down. You had to learn to take the bad along with the good.

Ordinarily, Nuala would have handed over complete responsibility for The Van to Paul when it came to anything mechanical. But she couldn't do that now. She was in this fix on her own and she had to sort it out.

'I can and I will,' she told herself through gritted teeth. She was a capable, independent woman. She'd known that taking this journey on her own would, at some point, present challenges. That was life, wasn't it? She just hadn't imagined a challenge would come this quickly.

Still there was an upside to The Van breaking down unexpectedly, she told herself. It was 'content'. She could turn the experience into a video. That should be an interesting subject for fellow van travellers, she thought, especially from the solo female perspective.

And with that positive spin on it, she turned the camera

on and had a little rant about it for her YouTube channel, getting some shots of the country lane she now found herself in and the very dead dashboard. Only then did she think she'd better try and get help.

She didn't like leaving The Van on the side of a road, but at least it was quiet and shouldn't cause any major problems for passing vehicles. She couldn't remember much about the village she'd just driven through. There'd been at least one shop and she was pretty sure she'd seen a garage but had it been open? And would they be able to help? A motorhome was a pretty specialised thing, but maybe they'd be able to get in touch with someone.

'*Quel* nightmare!' she cried. And then something else occurred to her. Would she be able to communicate with anyone?

'I guess I'm about to find out,' she said to herself.

When Laurie awoke bright and early for her day trip to the island of La Gomera, she had a huge smile on her face because she knew that the chartreuse dress was waiting on a hanger for her. She got out of bed and, just for a few moments, stared at its vivid colour against the dark of the dated hotel wardrobe. It filled Laurie with excitement just looking at it. It was the kind of dress that made a promise to its wearer: *Put me on and I will make sure your day is fabulous!*

Well, Laurie wasn't going to say no to that. Ever since her paragliding outing, she'd been struggling with the realisation that her marriage was over even though no actual conversation had taken place between her and Jeremy. All the indications were there in their behaviour towards each other and the atmosphere between them. It had slowly crept up on her and yet hadn't really hit her until she'd been up in the air paragliding towards the sea. She wondered why she'd felt it in that particular moment – mid-air above Tenerife. She knew that her body had been carrying the truth for some years even if her mind hadn't been willing to accept it. She'd felt the weight of it in every fibre and it showed in her sluggishness, her despondency, her weight gain and her apathy. It wasn't all down to the menopause – she was quite sure of that. She'd been carrying the heaviness of disappointment, of sadness, and of oh-so-many regrets.

Stroking the bright material of the new dress now, she determined to put any thoughts of her marriage firmly in her rear-view mirror. Today was going to be a day of exploration. She was leaving one island to visit another, crossing the sea on a fifty-minute boat ride. The coach was picking her up outside her hotel along with the other passengers and they would then proceed to the harbour for embarkation. When she'd booked the excursion, she'd been told to make sure that she had her passport with her as it would be checked before getting on the boat. How exciting! Laurie had so been looking forward to seeing La Gomera. She remembered asking Jeremy to book the excursion for them when they'd been in Tenerife together but, seeing as he hadn't even wanted to leave the resort town or even the hotel, there'd been no chance. Well, she was going now.

An hour later, having had a shower, blow-dried her hair, put on make-up and had breakfast wearing T-shirt and jeans, the moment had come. It was time to change into the dress. Even though it had been cheap enough to buy, it still looked too good for Laurie. It was just so new. She wasn't used to buying new clothes for herself. Marriage to penny pincher Jeremy had taught her to be frugal.

Quickly getting out of the very dull T-shirt and jeans combo which she had grown so used to over the years, she pulled the dress over her head and let it fall softly over her body. Oh, how wonderful it felt – so light and bright and sexy! She could practically feel her whole body blushing as she looked at her reflection. But there wasn't much of a chance to revel at her own reflection because it was time to leave for the coach pickup so she grabbed her light cotton cardigan and handbag.

It was as Laurie was climbing the steps into the coach just fifteen minutes later that she began to wonder if the new dress had been such a good idea after all. And when the tour guide Antonio told her where she was sitting, she began to regret her choice of attire even more. It turned out that Laurie was the only solo traveller on the coach that day. Everybody else was with a partner, friend or family.

'You're with the Rossi family from Italy,' Antonio told her. 'Do not move around the coach or it will disrupt everything.'

Laurie felt a bit taken aback by this. As if her movements alone could cause the utter disruption of the day. She really didn't think she possessed that much power, but maybe she did.

'Come with me,' he said, leading her down the aisle of the coach.' They were about half-way down when he motioned to a spare seat next to an absolutely enormous man wearing bright red shorts whose bare left knee was splayed across Laurie's seat at an alarming angle. The man – Mr Rossi she assumed – glanced up at her and nodded, but didn't shift in his seat to make room for her. Laurie did her best to squash herself into the seat assigned for her, her new dress barely covering her own knees. She did her best to pull it over them but the material wasn't very giving so she placed her handbag securely across them. It was going to be a very long day.

CHAPTER EIGHTEEN

Nuala had got lucky. Very lucky. There had, indeed, been a garage in the village she'd passed through just before The Van had broken down. Not only that but it was open and the owner knew of a mechanic who could help – at least he *hoped* he could help. No promises. It was specialised. It would be expensive and it would take as long as it took.

In her best schoolgirl French and with lots of help from Google Translate, she asked if there was anywhere nearby where she could stay.

The garage owner shook his head. But then added something with a dismissive shrug.

Had he said *chateau*?

He gave her directions and said something about a crazy lady. An American.

Well, she'd wanted to see more French chateaux. It's just that she hadn't expected this to be the way she'd do it.

She returned to The Van in the garage owner's vehicle, and quickly packed a few clothes, toiletries and her laptop as he examined things. She hated the thought of leaving her vehicle, but she had no choice and at least it would be in safe hands and off the road. Thank goodness she'd broken down near a garage and not on a busy motorway or in the middle of nowhere.

As she left The Van, she thanked him and he pointed down the road which would, she hoped, lead to some accommodation for her that night. The next thing to worry about would be if it was affordable. Weren't these places deluxe and expensive? She and Paul had never been ones to spend on luxurious accommodation. They usually hired cheap-as-chips self-catering places out of season or very brief city breaks in Europe. They'd been saving up for early retirement and 'The Big One'. So all those poky chalets on the windy Welsh coast and the dated B & Bs in middle of nowhere Cornwall would be worth it, they'd told themselves. That's how they'd been able to afford to buy The Van.

It felt funny walking down the country lane carrying her handbag, suitcase and laptop. A couple of cows in a field raised their heads, their liquid eyes showing no surprise – just curiosity. Nuala smiled.

'*Bonjour!*' she called over the gate. '*Le château est-il près d'ici?*' She shrugged. She guessed she was still heading in the right direction seeing as there was just one road.

She had her answer a few minutes later for, rounding a corner, she got her first glimpse of the chateau, sitting in golden splendour, its two gloriously fat turrets shooting into the blue sky above. Nuala marvelled at its great expanse of grey slate roof and was very glad she wasn't responsible for the upkeep of such a place, trying to imagine what an electricity bill would look like for such a sumptuous home. What on earth was an American doing here? As she reached the entrance, she hoped she'd find out but she wondered what she'd do if there was nobody at home as there were no cars in front of the building

Her feet crunched over the gravel driveway. She noticed a few weeds and a low wall nearby that was crumbling, a piece of rope stopping visitors from using the path next to it. Nuala walked up the shallow steps to the enormous front door under a very fine porch held aloft with fluted columns. There was a wonderfully old-fashioned bell which you pulled and she gave it a good yank.

Once.

Twice.

Three times.

There was no answer.

She walked around the front of the building, peering into the windows. The paintwork was flaking, but the glass was clean and there were pretty curtains hanging inside. There was no sign of anyone there – owner nor guests.

Nuala would have to wait if she wanted to find out if she could stay here and it certainly looked like a fun place to hide away for a few days. This van business could actually be a blessing in disguise, she couldn't help thinking. With the heat she was feeling from Paul and all the social media coverage, she was beginning to get anxious that people might actually try to track her down. She'd checked her YouTube channel again before leaving The Van in the capable hands of the garage owner, and she'd had a few messages from people wanting to meet up with her on the road. Others had reportedly spotted her. It was much too much attention and might help Paul find her. Nuala had never expected this when she'd started her little channel. She supposed that, even if she took the viral video down, it would be too late. The damage had been done and she'd been flabbergasted to see that other people had posted her video elsewhere or else edited highlights from it and used it in hurtful ways in their own content. What was wrong with the world? Couldn't a menopausal woman have a public rant in peace?

Anyway, this forced pause in her plans might be just what she needed to regroup. She smiled. Could a solo traveller "regroup"?

She looked around for somewhere to sit and spotted a beautiful one-storey building nearby. An orangery, Nuala guessed. She could always take shelter in there if it rained. The sky was looking as if it hadn't quite made its mind up as to whether it was going to plump for storm or sunshine. But it was pleasantly warm and Nuala found a wrought iron bench to sit on, placing her things next to her. She sighed. Was she officially homeless? What if The Van couldn't be fixed? Or what if the garage was corrupt and sold it? What if she was stranded in the middle of France with just one suitcase and a laptop?

No, no, no! She was looking at this the wrong way. It was just going to take a bit of time. And Nuala was now officially a woman of leisure. Time was on her side at last. She kept having to remind herself that. She didn't have to be anywhere or report to anyone. The only timetable she had was the one she imposed on herself and she could easily change that at a moment's notice. That was the beauty of being retired.

It was also the beauty of being solo, she thought. There was nobody here to tell her where they should go next and by which route. She had to admit that was something of a relief. She enjoyed the little daily decisions she made on her own: choosing where to go and where to stop, what to see and when to eat. It sounded simple enough but, when you'd lived so many years as one half of a couple, it became second nature to always ask or check or compromise.

Had Nuala been asked just a couple of months ago how she'd feel about being single and making all the decisions herself, she would have panicked. It would be too much to take on. There'd be too many options each day for one person. Too much responsibility. She couldn't have done it. And yet here she was doing it – and doing it well. Apart from finding herself vanless in the middle of France, that was. But it amazed her that she'd been so resilient and that she'd coped with what life had thrown at her. Sure, there'd been tears and a couple of meltdowns, but that was normal. Oh, and the public rant, but that was normal for these days too, wasn't it? For what was the point of having an emotion if you didn't share it with the entire world?

From her wrought iron seat, Nuala rested her eyes on the chateau. She wondered if the owner had a YouTube channel. Many did these days. She'd watched a few episodes of a TV show once that followed chateau owners as they bought and restored old shells that had been left to rot in the French countryside. Curiously, none of the owners were French. It just seemed to be crazy Brits, Canadians and Americans who fell for the romantic dream of living in a chateau. Nuala couldn't help wondering what had made this particular American seek out a corner of France to call her own. She hoped she'd get to find out.

Nuala had been waiting for about half an hour when an old Citroen drove up the driveway and came to a stop outside the chateau. Nuala got up from her seat and, leaving her suitcase and laptop just in case she wasn't invited inside, went to greet the driver, hoping it would be the owner.

She watched as a small woman with short curly white-blonde hair got out of the car. She looked a little older than Nuala and wore a pair of glasses on a chain around her neck.

'Bonjour!' Nuala called, hoping she wouldn't startle the woman as she wasn't sure she'd seen her.

'Bonjour,' the woman replied, turning and giving Nuala an appraising look. 'English, are you?'

'Yes – well, half Irish!' Nuala was impressed that she'd been able to gauge that from just one word but not really surprised as she hadn't ever been able to master the French accent no matter how many apps she'd tried on her phone or numerous YouTube videos she'd watched.

'Well, you're in luck because I'm American!'

Nuala smiled. 'I'm Nuala.'

'Lindy.'

They shook hands.

'Are you the owner?'

'I am.'

'Because I'm looking for somewhere to stay.'

'Well, I'm not sure I can help,' Lindy began.

'Oh dear!'

'Seeing as I've only got the seven vacant rooms,' Lindy finished.

'Oh!' Nuala laughed in relief.

'Last-minute cancellation so you're in luck.'

'What a relief! My motorhome broke down just outside the village so I'm homeless for a while.'

'Ah! I wondered how you'd got here. Get your bags and follow me!'

Nuala ran back to the bench to grab her things and followed Lindy into the chateau.

'Door's a bit sticky,' she said, giving it a good shove with her shoulder. 'When I first got the keys for the place, I couldn't get in for at least ten minutes so this is a definite improvement.'

Nuala grinned and then gasped as she crossed the threshold into the entrance hall: a room filled with light and a large sweep of staircase straight ahead of her.

'This place is amazing!'

'There's still a lot to do. But it's hard to know what to prioritise when *everything* needs doing, right?'

Nuala nodded. 'How long have you been here?'

'Nine years now.'

'And what sort of state was the chateau in when you bought it?'

'Well, it had been empty for twelve years and neglected for many more before that. There were birds roosting in the bedrooms and cobwebs where there should have been curtains. That should give you some idea.'

She led the way up the impressive staircase, passing a number of old portraits.

'Were these past owners?' Nuala asked.

'I shouldn't think so. I got them from the charity shop Emmaus!'

Nuala laughed. 'They look very at home here.'

'Yes, I think so too.'

They'd reached the landing now.

'You're here alone?' Lindy asked.

'Yes.'

'All the rooms are about the same size, but we do have a family room with a double bed and two single.'

'A normal is fine.'

'All are en suite. There's nothing worse than having to leave the privacy of your own room in the middle of the night for a trip to the bathroom, is there?'

Nuala nodded in agreement.

'I think this room might suit you,' Lindy said, stopping to open a door to her right. 'It has a lovely view over the garden and gets the morning light.'

Nuala followed her inside and sighed appreciatively. The room was a delight to the eye. A great wrought iron bed sat at its centre with pretty pink-and-white toile de Jouy bedding and a heap of coordinated pillows and cushions, with matching curtains at the window. The walls were a soft creamy white and everything was beautiful and elegant. It was the sort of room that featured in expensive glossy magazines or coffee table books.

Nuala panicked. 'I don't think I can afford this.'

Lindy shook her head. 'Listen, I probably shouldn't be telling you this, but I've barely seen a guest for weeks. I did have this party of ten booked but then they cancelled. So you can pay what you want and that'll be fine.'

'Really?'

'Truly. Or maybe we can come to some arrangement. Are you any good with a paintbrush?'

Nuala laughed. 'Not bad. I've painted my share of walls over the years.'

'Awesome!'

Nuala felt it was time to be honest. 'I'm not sure how long I'll be here,' she confessed. 'My van – it's really annoying as I've just got it. And I haven't gone very far really. I mean, I've driven from the UK, but that's hardly Mars, is it? Although my husband – my *ex* – has something to say about that! Anyway, I'm not sure what's happening really. Does that make sense?' She laughed and then wondered why she'd shared quite so much. She hadn't meant to, but maybe it was the novelty of talking to a real live person at last instead of just a camera screen.

Lindy was staring at her and Nuala began to feel anxious, but then her host gasped in recognition. 'You're her, aren't you?'

'Who?'

'The ranting RV woman!' Lindy's hands flew to her mouth. 'Sorry... I mean – your video...'

'You've seen it?'

'It's really you? I didn't recognise you.'

Nuala cleared her throat. 'Yes, well my hair's a little less wild now and... I've calmed down a bit.' She self-consciously patted her hair down.

The two women stared at one another for a moment before bursting into laughter.

'I can't believe it!' Lindy said. 'Right here in my chateau! I mean, you're *here*!'

'I am!' Nuala said, feeling a little nonplussed by the response she was getting. 'How did you see the video?'

'I can't remember, but it's everywhere!'

'What do you mean?'

'People are talking about it on all the socials. You can't avoid it – whatever platform you're on.'

'Oh, dear!'

'You're a sensation!'

'I didn't mean to be.' Nuala got her phone out and quickly brought up her YouTube channel. The view count that greeted her nearly knocked her over.

'It's got over three million views! How's that happened? I only put it up two days ago.'

'Well, you've got people's attention and it's being shared. Something's resonating with folk.'

'This is crazy!' Nuala perched on the end of the bed and Lindy sat down next to her.

'You'll have to make the most of it. Is your channel monetised yet?'

'I've no idea.'

'You'll have to get on to that. You can earn through the ads played during your videos and you're getting a lot of plays.'

'Right!' Nuala said, wondering how she'd missed this trick and how wonderful it would be to have a source of income again to supplement her modest private pension. 'How do you know all this?'

'I started a channel about buying this place but that market's pretty saturated. "Mad American buys dilapidated French chateau" – it's a bit commonplace now and I think people are fed up with it. I had a couple of videos do well. Some even got me bookings, but it's a lot of work on top of everything else I was doing and I'm afraid I've let it slide. But never mind about me. What are you going to do?'

'What do you mean?'

'You've got all these people watching you. Don't you want to do something with that?'

Nuala's mouth dropped open. 'I don't know. I haven't really thought about it.'

'All those views and subscribers – you could be selling something to them. A guide to life after separation maybe. Or a tour guide of Europe in a van.'

'I'm not sure I'm qualified to do anything like that.'

Lindy stood up. 'Well, think about it. An opportunity like this doesn't land in everybody's lap.'

CHAPTER NINETEEN

It wasn't the first time Elise had woken several times in the night nor was it the first time she'd got to a certain point and had given up hope of falling back to sleep. It was, she realised, one of the many joys of being menopausal. She'd been having symptoms for three years now and some were definitely more disruptive than others. Restless sleep was not one of her favourites – that was for sure. She would wake up with her whole body burning and have to get up immediately in order to cool down, drinking cold water and then washing her face, hands and arms to restore her body temperature as best as she could. Thankfully, since starting HRT, the night sweats had subsided, but she found that her sleep patterns were still disturbed.

She looked at her little travel clock. She'd had what – six hours of sleep, tops? Was that enough? She felt okay. That was something which had surprised her at first. She'd thought she'd feel more drained with losing so much sleep, but she was still able to do everything in a day that she needed to. So maybe she should start looking at it as a kind of superpower. She could certainly make the most of her extra hours of consciousness in Italy. And at least she had more time to take care of herself these days.

While her mother had been alive, Elise had always put her own health worries to one side; she simply hadn't had the time or energy to take proper care of both her mother and herself as well as holding down her job and doing all the necessary things that a single woman had to do to keep a house running. But, since her mother had died, she'd been able to address her own needs and it had been remarkable what a difference it had made: getting herself the medication she needed, taking time away from work and listening to her own body. The rush of the modern world could often leave people with so little time in which to prioritise what was important – the foundations of their health both mental and physical. Elise was already noticing the difference since she'd made time for herself and, when she looked back at the woman she'd been a year ago, it made her realise just how bad things had been, and that made her more determined than ever to make the very best of the here and now.

She couldn't believe that her time in Florence was coming to an end. She'd spent her last two full days following Great Aunt Clara's sketchbooks and finding the most delightful details in the city she might have otherwise missed from beautiful doorways and tiny churches to a curve in a backstreet and a view across the Arno. She'd done well to find most of the places her aunt had sketched. She'd loved being a part of the city for the month and wondered if she should have booked her apartment for longer and if there might be an option to do so now. But there were other places in Italy she wanted to see – so many others. It was the traveller's dilemma, she quickly realised: do you explore more places quickly or do fewer in more depth? Elise was hoping that her travels would afford both opportunities.

She'd spent hours poring over maps of Italy and wondering which direction to go in from Florence. It made most sense to head south because Europe's south would be heating up as the months progressed towards summer and Elise knew that, although she adored the Mediterranean, she was – alas – an English woman with an English woman's pale complexion which turned from white to red as soon as the summer sun had shone for two consecutive days.

She had long had a fascination for Puglia because of the iconic *trulli* houses and so she'd departed from following Great Aunt Clara and treated herself to a stay in one in the countryside surrounding Alberobello. That meant she'd had to book a local hire a car to explore the area – a terrifying prospect to her. It was also a seven-hour train ride to get there, but Elise preferred the idea of a train rather than the hassle of an airport and planes.

She was excited to see more of Italy, but – oh! The temptation to stay in *Firenze*! Still, if she stayed in Florence, she knew she risked losing her nerve and becoming a bit too comfortable and that – heaven forbid – Florence would then start to lose its edge. She didn't ever believe that she'd come to take such a beautiful city for granted, but she was already beginning to speed walk through the city to get to places. Just the other day, she'd been on her way to find a church and couldn't actually remember crossing the Ponte Vecchio en route. Wasn't that terrible? Maybe that was her cue to leave. She had followed in the footsteps of E M Forster's characters, she had found most of the sights which her Great Aunt Clara had sketched, and – perhaps most importantly – she'd discovered the city for herself too. In short, she'd absorbed as much beauty as was humanly possible and it was time to move on – to see new places and experience new things.

It was sad packing everything away. This little apartment had been such a wonderful haven and Elise knew that she'd be leaving it quite a different person from the one who had arrived. It had given her the time and space she'd needed to simply be – becoming a home if only for a few short weeks. She thought back to the woman she'd been at the airport, terrified of venturing out into the world and worrying that she'd made a horrible mistake, and yet something had urged her forward. It was as if a deeper part of her had known she could blossom and bloom. She'd just needed to take that first scary step and she was so glad that she had.

She took her clothes out of the tiny wardrobe and chest of drawers, stroking the fine fabrics of the new pieces she'd bought from the boutique she'd revisited. She'd chosen the gorgeous top in dusky pink which she'd reached for the day she'd met Andie, a lovely soft burgundy scarf, a caramel-coloured jumper and a new pair of jeans. It had been years since Elise had worn jeans and she'd believed that she was too old for them now but the sales assistant had been very persuasive and Elise had to admit that they looked good on her and were surprisingly comfortable too.

So much for travelling light. But maybe she could sort out some of the tired old clothes she'd brought with her. There was nothing much she liked from her old wardrobe and perhaps it was time to shed them all – a bit like a snake sheds its skin when its outgrown it. This could be Elise's great shedding and renewal.

It was when she was in the bathroom tidying her things away that she saw a glint of metal in her make-up bag. She brought out the silver bangle and examined it under the strip light above the mirror which made it shine. It had belonged to her mother and Elise wasn't quite sure why she'd brought it with her. It wasn't particularly pretty nor was it valuable and she certainly hadn't been planning on wearing it. Still she couldn't resist trying it on now, turning her wrist around to admire the silver simplicity of the piece. She didn't think it was very old and she really couldn't remember her mother wearing it. Her mother hadn't been a great one for jewellery and Elise had only found a few cheap bead necklaces and some rather dull stud earrings in her bedside cabinet. And this silver bangle.

Elise turned it around and around on her slim wrist. She never wore bracelets or bangles, finding them rather cold as well as impractical with the neat cuffed and buttoned blouses she wore to work.

She walked into the living room to see the bangle in daylight by the window and was immediately struck that it resembled a handcuff. The symbolism was so overpowering and she instantly knew she couldn't keep it. She also knew what she was going to do with it.

Popping a light jacket on as it was a little cloudy, Elise left her apartment for one last walk into the centre of Florence before leaving. She had a very particular spot in mind.

She walked through the streets that had become so familiar to her now, nodding at Bruno the owner of her favourite café as she passed. She crossed the Ponte Vecchio, taking in the open wooden shutters revealing the gold-filled jewellers' windows. It was such a pretty sight but she wasn't stopping to look at it today. She was on a mission. It did occur to her that she might be able to sell the bangle but she didn't expect it would be worth much and the Florentine jewellers would probably just laugh and sniff at the cheap bauble. She'd had a good look at the price tags on some of the pieces they were selling and it was quite shocking.

Leaving the bridge, she turned right along the River Arno until she found the spot she'd visited on her first day in Florence – the place where Julian Sands and Helena Bonham Carter had stood in the film adaptation of *A Room with a View*. It was the spot where George, played by Julian Sands, had thrown a packet of photographs into the swirling waters of the Arno after they'd been damaged in an incident in the Piazza della Signoria.

Now, as Elise stood in the same spot, she was quite sure what she was about to do was the right thing. She looked down at her wrist, noticing how the silver bangle seemed to constrict her like a hungry snake. It was something of a relief to take it off and, without giving it anymore thought, she threw it into the river, watching the silver blue waters in fear that it might resurface. But of course it didn't. The river had accepted what she'd rejected and its removal left her feeling just a little bit lighter.

She stood for a moment longer, her gaze softening as her resolve hardened. She was leaving something of the old Elise here, she was sure of that.

It was time to move on.

There was no denying that La Gomera was one of the most beautiful places Laurie had ever seen. The lush landscape with its deep valleys and jutting rock formations and roads twisting up into ancient laurel forests simply took her breath away. It was truly an island that time had forgotten and she wouldn't have been at all surprised if a dinosaur casually walked across the road.

But what wasn't so lovely was the coach itself: the air conditioning was definitely substandard and it soon became an overfilled and uncomfortable metal container. Her travel companion Mr Rossi still encroached into her personal space. Laurie had offered him the aisle seat – believing he'd be more comfortable there and also able to speak more easily to his wife and daughter without talking across her which she thought very rude indeed. But no – he insisted on monopolising the window seat.

Laurie determined she'd be the first back on the coach after their next stop and she'd claim the window seat. After all, she'd paid for her ticket just as he had. It was only fair that they shared the window.

Luckily, the next stop was the small island's capital San Sebastián, where they had a bit of time to walk around and see the sights. Laurie was grateful to get off the coach and escape the Rossi family and she enjoyed exploring the pretty streets lined with their distinctive Canarian buildings – many were white with burgundy or brown painted windows and glorious balconies, while others were pretty yellows and reds. It really was a delightful place and Laurie quickly decided that it was her new favourite capital because it was just so small and quiet. It was also surprisingly warm. For a little while, as the coach had taken them into the hills, the sun had been swallowed up by cloud and the temperature had dropped, but it was sunny again now and Laurie determined to find a café.

She made her way to the main square where she discovered the most glorious laurel trees. Their huge grey trunks shot high into the sky and their dark green leaves provided much welcome shade to the lucky occupants of the benches beneath.

Laurie found a café and ordered a large fruit smoothie, relieved that she didn't recognise anyone else from her coach tour. They all seemed to have dispersed or found other cafés or places to grab a bite to eat after the rather awful lunch they'd been given at the restaurant in the hills. Laurie still wasn't quite sure what she'd eaten – or rather what she'd attempted to eat. It seemed to be a thin soup full of stones. She shook her head, trying to dispel the memory and that's when she became aware of a young man who seemed to be staring at her from the next table but one. She looked across at him and he smiled warmly at her. Or was it at somebody behind her? Laurie glanced round. But there was just an elderly couple chatting to one another over some tapas.

When she looked back, the young man was still smiling at her. No, it was more than smiling – it was flirting. She was quite sure of it. And he was very handsome, she couldn't help thinking, so she began to flirt back. She gave a little flick of her hair and the smallest of smiles. Gosh, she hadn't flirted for years. It was a wonder she still knew how to do it and yet she did and it felt good. A little bubble of excitement grew inside her as the young man smiled again. She liked this game. A game of smiles. A gentle appreciation of one another.

She really didn't expect anymore than that and was genuinely surprised – maybe even a little shocked – when the young man got up from his seat and approached her table, his smile even wider than before.

'*Hola!* I'm Santiago,' he said. 'But you can call me Santi.' He motioned to the empty seat at her table and she nodded.

'I'm Laurie.'

'*Hola* Laurie. *Encantado.*'

He reached across the table and they shook hands.

He was Spanish, he told her, with a little Italian thrown in for good measure. Laurie watched him as he spoke – his dark eyes sparkled with mischief and his hand gestures were so full of life and energy.

She told him where she was staying, wondering if it was wise to let him know that she was on her own and – when she told him she was with a tour group and had to get back on a coach in a little while, he frowned at her.

'I have a better way,' he told her, motioning towards a motorbike. 'Come with me!'

'What?'

'Forget your boring coach tour. I'll give you a tour of the island.'

'I can't just abandon my group!'

'Why not? You're a grown woman,' he said and she was quite sure he gave her entire body an appreciative glance. 'You can do what you want.'

'But I don't know you!'

'What do you want to know? I'm Santi. I am a citizen of the world. I travel. I make my own way. I like food and bikes and beautiful women from England.'

She laughed. His enthusiasm for life, for La Gomera, and – perhaps most importantly – for her was infectious. And oh, that smile of his!

Santi glanced up at the sky. 'The sun won't smile forever, Laurie,' he told her as he kicked one of his biker boots against the other. He was ready to leave. 'Are you coming with me?'

There were so many reasons why she should say no. She was so much older than him. He was a total stranger. She was still married. And the old Laurie who used to work in a grey office would never say yes to such an invitation. But the new Laurie in her fabulous chartreuse dress so wanted to have this adventure. She deserved it, didn't she?

And so she nodded. '*Si!*'

Santi laughed.

'Just give me one moment,' she added.

Laurie had spotted her tour guide Antonio going into a bar off the main square after he'd let the group loose in San Sebastián. She was hoping he'd still be there and was pleased to see him chatting animatedly to the bartender as she entered.

'Can I have a word?' she asked.

'Sure. Everything okay?'

She nodded, suddenly feeling like a naughty schoolgirl who was about to tell a massive lie to get out of class.

'If it's okay with you, I won't be joining the group again.'

Antonio frowned. 'Are you unwell?'

'No. It's just...' she paused. She couldn't very well tell him she was taking off with a biker who was young enough to be her son, could she? Well, she could, she supposed. In fact, a part of her would have loved to have seen his reaction. But she was a grown woman and so she lied.

'I'd like to do my own thing – explore.'

'But you'll miss out on the rest of what you've paid for.'

'That's okay. I'm happy... here.'

The guide didn't look convinced.

'And the coach – the roads – were making me feel a bit dizzy,' Laurie added for good measure.

'Ah, yes! They can have that effect,' he said, nodding. He'd obviously heard that before. 'I will need a message from you to say you will be leaving the tour group.' He pulled out his phone and Laurie quickly sent him a message on

WhatsApp. He nodded his approval. 'Make sure you have plenty of water and a rest, yes? And you'll be on the ferry?'

'Of course.'

'And on the coach for drop off later?'

Laurie bit her lip. She didn't want to commit to that. As far as she was concerned, she never wanted to get on that coach again.

'I'll walk from the ferry. It's not far to my hotel. It'll be quicker.'

'You're sure?'

She nodded. 'Thank you. It's been a lovely day.'

He smiled and turned back to the bartender. She was free to go.

Santi was waiting for her by his bike. 'Are you coming?'

She gave a nervous smile and he handed her a helmet. She took it, carefully picking out a long red hair from inside and noticing a distinct smell of perfume. She wouldn't ask him whose that was. She watched as he opened one of the panniers on the back of the bike.

'You've been on a bike before?' he asked.

'Yes, but it was a long time ago.'

'I take care of you, Laurie. Put these on.' He handed her trousers, gloves and a jacket.

'You have spare everything?'

'Of course. It's safer for making friends.'

Laurie was glad he was conscientious when carrying a passenger. After all, her new flimsy summer dress was definitely not conducive to riding even a pushbike.

As she popped the protective clothes on as modestly as she could in the middle of the street, she watched as he shrugged his shoulders into his own jacket and put his helmet on.

'I should just say...' Laurie began hesitantly, 'that I don't like speed.'

Santi held his gloved hands out in an open gesture. 'I don't like speed either.'

She couldn't tell if he was telling the truth now that his visor was down but she was dressed for adventure, wasn't she? And she'd feel an absolute fool going back to the coach having excused herself from it.

'I'm trusting you,' she told him as she hopped on the bike behind him.

'*Muy bien!*' he said. 'Good! I'm very trustworthy!'

She took a deep breath before closing her own visor and holding on to the grab rails.

What on earth am I doing?

The little voice in Laurie's head was drowned out as the bike started up and, with a great whoosh, they were off, leaving San Sebastián behind them and heading ever upwards into the hills of La Gomera.

It was years since Laurie had ridden a motorbike and she was glad she was wearing her sturdy trainers and not the insubstantial shoes she'd first teemed with her new dress. She looked down at the flutter of her hem against the biker trousers he'd given her to wear. The clothes were a little big for her but they were cosy against the wind they were riding through and the sudden pockets of mist that circled the island's roads. At first, she held on to the grab rails so tightly that she knew her knuckles were white within the gloves, but she slowly relaxed a little and actually began to enjoy herself. And she remembered to lean with Santi when he took the corners rather than remaining upright. The trick was to become part of the bike rather than cargo.

Scenes from her early twenties flashed into her mind. A

young man named Ed who'd fixed a vintage bike he'd picked up for next to nothing. They'd had so many adventures on that together. Laurie remembered how they'd sped down country lanes, terrifying the wildlife. And how they'd stopped in picturesque places so he could photograph his beloved vehicle. He'd definitely taken more photos of the bike than of her, Laurie remembered with a grin.

She wondered what had happened to Ed. Was he still fixing and riding vintage motorbikes? Or had he settled down into a dull, predictable life in an office somewhere? Life had a habit of swallowing people whole, didn't it? Maybe that's why she was on the back of Santi's bike now. It was all part of her reclaiming her life and feeling something of that spirit that had been slowly eroded over the years.

As she caught a glimpse of the sea in the distance, she wondered why she'd stopped allowing herself moments like this. Not that young men like Santi came striding into her life every day and she had to bat them away. But rather when had she accepted that life didn't need moments like this? That it was okay to simply work, work, work? When had she signed that deal?

Laurie determined not to fall down that particular rabbit hole of self-pity. She had to remember the teachings of her recent yoga retreat.

All we have is the present moment.

Come back to your breath.

Just breathe.

Controlling her breath also helped with the slight panic as Santi took some particularly hairy corners with terrifying drops. She did her best not to tense but focused on his shoulders, moving with him and the bike and controlling her fear. She had chosen to be here and to hand over control to this young man and she was determined to enjoy the experience.

Seeing La Gomera from the back of a bike felt so completely different from being next to a fat Italian window-seat hog on a coach. She might not have coach-height views, but the ground rushing beneath her made her feel so much more alive. She wasn't just drifting around the island – she was a part of it.

Santi kept his word too – he didn't speed and he took the corners carefully. He also pointed out a few views for Laurie to enjoy. After about fifteen minutes, Santi pulled over in a lay-by at one of the famous viewpoints on the island by Roque de Agando – the massive rock formation that looked like a kind of rounded tower rising out of the landscape. They got off the bike and removed their helmets.

'How was it?' Santi asked her.

Laurie felt quite breathless and she didn't altogether trust her legs to keep her upright.

'Brilliant!'

He grinned. 'Bien! We can go faster now if you like.'

'Oh, no!' Laurie shook her head.

'Okay!' He held his hands up. 'I take your picture, *si*?'

'*Si*!' Laurie posed for him against the bike, feeling a little self-conscious with her dress fluttering over the trousers he'd given her to wear. Did she look silly? Her hair felt like a mess and the sun on her face was probably highlighting every single line around her eyes and her mouth. Maybe she shouldn't smile. Maybe smiling would give her age away and Santi would realise with sudden horror that he had an old lady riding on his bike. But she smiled nevertheless because he was grinning at her with such warmth and enthusiasm and telling her to pose.

'Hand on hip, Laurie!'

She laughed, feeling that all the other tourists who'd stopped to take photos were looking at her, judging her. But she did it anyway. She put her hand on her hip and smiled and it felt great. When was the last time Jeremy had taken a photo of her, she couldn't help wondering. And the fact that she couldn't answer that question made her feel very sad. Mind you, she hadn't wanted to take any of him either, had she?

'Your turn!' she said to Santi, getting her phone out of her bag.

They switched positions and Santi posed for her. He was a natural. He just looked so cool.

And young!

He also had the kind of confidence that was impossible to ignore. It was quite magnetic. More so, perhaps, than his looks which, in themselves, were enough to turn heads. But the package of the two was absolutely devastating.

Laurie swallowed hard and concentrated on getting a few good shots of him. They then swapped phones and did the whole thing again, including taking a fair few selfies. Now that was something she and Jeremy had *never* done.

They then spent a few moments gazing out into the vastness of the green valley below them. It was such an incredible landscape and it felt like an honour to be standing there in that moment feeling so very small and yet, at the same time, harbouring such huge emotions. This, Laurie thought, was what she'd hoped for from travel – this feeling of peace and awe and gratitude.

She turned to look at Santi and he was pointing out across the landscape towards the coast. A rainbow arched across the valley in the distance, casting a magical light.

Laurie felt tears threatening and did her best to hide them by picking up her phone and taking a few photos. Santi was standing very close to her.

'So beautiful,' he said and she nodded as she took one more photo before turning to face him.

And she saw that Santi wasn't looking at the rainbow. He was looking at her.

CHAPTER TWENTY

Elise was pretty tired by the time she reached her destination. The long train ride from Florence had exhausted her. She'd enjoyed the ever-changing scenery, but the constant noise of her fellow passengers had really taken it out of her. She'd be glad to enjoy the peace of Puglia at last.

The Villa Trullo Gianna was a one-bedroomed whitewashed building with a conical-shaped roof made of grey slate. A modern extension had been added to provide a kitchen, sitting area and small shower room. Elise knew that the area was famous for its trulli houses and she was so excited to see them. They were like something out of a fairytale and Elise was instantly smitten although she felt a little guilty for having booked such a luxurious place just for herself. It came with its own pool and spacious outside area where there were two sun loungers, an outdoor shower and a barbeque.

She still hadn't quite got used to the concept of spoiling herself and being comfortable with the fact that she could afford to splurge every so often. After all, she'd denied herself such pleasures for years. Decades. So why was she feeling so guilty now?

She'd made the booking online and she'd swapped a few messages with the owner via WhatsApp. Elise had let her know her rough time of arrival and she was pleased to have made good time since picking up the hire car. She'd only taken one wrong turn down an adjacent dead-end lane which meant she'd had to reverse the car into an olive grove. Luckily, there had been nobody around to witness her embarrassment other than a lizard watching her from a stone wall.

When she finally found the place, she pulled up and got out, stretching her arms up to the sky and marvelling at how warm it still was at five in the afternoon. She swore she hadn't seen a single cloud since leaving central Italy behind. Oh, how she could get used to a Mediterranean climate. After years of grey skies and erratic English summers, it felt so good to feel warm and to get up in the mornings and put the simplest, lightest of clothes on and to free her limbs to the elements.

She was just taking a closer look at the swimming pool and wondering how cold it was when a woman pulled up in a small white Fiat and got out. She had long dark hair tied back in a ponytail and her face was deeply tanned.

'Julia?' Elise said, walking towards the driveway to meet her.

'Elise?'

'*Piacere!*' Elise managed and Julia burst into a torrent of Italian to which Elise could only nod and smile.

'Would you prefer me to speak English?' Julia asked, responding to Elise's obvious puzzlement.

'Yes please. I am trying to become fluent, but it might take some time!'

'That's okay. I'm English.'

'I thought I detected an accent!'

'Born and bred in Cambridge.'

'Well, you sound very Italian.'

'I've gone native.'

'Have you lived here long?'

'Just two years but it feels like a lifetime. I actually came here – to the trullo – on holiday and...' she flapped her hands. 'You don't want to hear all that.'

'Oh, I absolutely do!'

Julia pursed her lips. 'Really?'

Elise nodded. She really did.

'Well, I'll give you time to settle in and, if you're not otherwise engaged this evening, come up to the farmhouse for dinner with us and I'll tell you everything then. Our place is just up the track. You can't miss it.'

'That's very kind of you.'

Julia smiled and Elise felt an immediate connection to this woman from her home country and couldn't help being intensely curious about her story.

It didn't take long to settle in after Julia had given her a quick tour of the trullo. Elise showered and changed and took her great aunt's sketchbook out to browse through while sitting on one of the sun loungers. It wasn't long before she realised she was being watched. By another lizard. It was such a delightful surprise to see the green-backed creature that she laughed, marvelling at how skinny it was and how its long tail curled over the wall it was resting on. It was the second one she'd seen that day and it made her wonder how many were around. She definitely wasn't in the England anymore.

That evening, she found her way to the farmhouse. It was a lovely walk along the track flanked by ancient olive groves – the shapes of the trees twisted by time. The sun was still bewitchingly warm and Elise was wearing a summer dress although she was carrying a cardigan in case it cooled down later.

She allowed herself a 'pinch me' moment, standing still by a low stone wall and gazing into the trees which rose out of the red earth.

I'm in Puglia, she told herself. *I've got myself all the way down to the south of Italy. The heel of the boot.*

It was still a miracle to her that she'd even left her home town, but to also have ventured out of the UK and made it to Italy was still mind-blowingly brilliant to her. And to be a witness to so much beauty. It was here all along and she'd never seen it. All she'd had to do was to summon the courage to leave home and go out and see it all. She had not had a single moment of regret since taking a break from her job or her home. Indeed, she wondered whether she ever wanted to return. There wasn't anything tying her to the place now. She could go anywhere she wanted. The thought of that made her quite giddy, but it was a little overwhelming too. Too much choice, she acknowledged. The whole world lay open to her just waiting for her to make her mind up.

She shook her head. In all likelihood, she'd return home. At some point. She'd chosen to buy an open return ticket because she really hadn't known how long her quest would take her and she'd wanted to lose herself in the experience of it all without having to time the journey. And, when the time finally came to return to the UK, she would sell her property in her home town. A change would do her good. In fact, now she thought about it, she was angry with herself for never having thought of doing it before. That small rebellion of even moving into a different county might have just been enough to shake things up a bit.

Elise had spent more than her fair share of time imagining alternative lives for herself over the years – wondering if a well-placed "yes" here or a defiant "no" there might have changed the trajectory of her life. Might she have met the love of her life if she'd moved to a different county? Might she be a mother to one or two or even more loving children now?

She shook her head, acknowledging the fact that these flights of fancy were always so unrealistic. Mind you – why shouldn't they be? You weren't going to fantasise about finding 'Mr He'll Do', were you? Or having three unappreciative children who hated you. Most people, when they imagined all the 'if only' scenarios, painted a rosy picture for themselves with the perfect partner, the adoring children, and the house and job of their dreams. Alternate lives were always faultless; they were never duplicates of what already was because what would be the point of that?

She sighed.

She wasn't going to think of that on this glorious evening. The future – whatever hers might be – could wait for her a little longer. She had dinner with new friends to look forward to and she was excited to learn more about what had brought Julia to Puglia!

~

Nuala woke up in the pink-and-white toile de Jouy room with a huge smile on her face. She'd slept very well indeed. As much as she loved The Van, she had to admit that it had felt good to sleep in a proper bed in a normal room again. With a normal en suite too. There was room to move around – to stretch your legs without going outside. She didn't have to worry about people looking in her windows or even tapping on them or kicking a ball against her door as one teenager had done repeatedly on a campsite in Devon.

She walked down the very grand staircase into the spacious entrance hall and found her way to the breakfast room. She might have been the only guest but Lindy had obviously gone to some effort to make the central table look picture perfect with beautiful white crockery against a pale pink tablecloth and single stem vases running down its centre, each with a tiny flower inside.

Nuala walked over to the enormous window to admire the curtains. How on earth did you begin to furnish a chateau, she wondered as she ran her hand down the soft drape of the fabric. She remembered having curtains made for her and Paul's bedroom with its very modest-sized suburban window. It had cost an eye-watering amount that had made Nuala gasp. Now, looking around this room at the three floor-to-ceiling windows, she could only imagine the bill. And this was just one room of many. Then there was the floor. This room had a beautiful pair of rugs either side of the centrally placed table. And the actual furniture and lighting. All that expense before you even factored in the cost of running everything.

As she was mulling all this over, Lindy entered the room.

'Did you sleep well?' her host asked as she placed a large

floral tray on the table laden with fruit, croissants, toast, boiled eggs, fruit juice and a teapot.

'I did. Very well,' Nuala said honestly, sitting down at the table, reaching for the teapot and pouring herself a cup. 'It was funny having a normal bed again.'

'Don't you have one in your vehicle?'

'Oh, I do, but it all feels so crowded sleeping in the same place as you shower, cook and drive.'

'Well, I'm glad you were comfortable. I chose the beds specially. There's nothing more irksome than a bad bed.'

'So how did you come to buy this place?' Nuala asked, starting with one of the boiled eggs and buttering herself a slice of toast.

'I got caught up in all those TV shows about folks buying and doing up French chateaux. It looked – achievable. I thought, if that funny old couple from Guerneville in California can make a go of it, why not me? I had a nest egg, determination and an eye for decoration. How hard could it be?'

Nuala motioned for Lindy to sit at the table with her. She wanted to hear this story. Lindy obliged.

'I don't know what made me do it. I've never been a dreamer, you see. I'm a practical person and used to work in management. But, when I hit fifty, something happened. You can call it menopause, or a mid-life crisis, but I think that's reductive and just plain lazy thinking. It was more a need to grasp life – to have an adventure. A real adventure. I thought about travelling but that all seemed a bit daunting on my own. Which is why I admire what you're doing so much.'

Nuala smiled. 'I'm afraid it was forced upon me.'

'That doesn't matter. You're still doing it! You could have

stayed at home, couldn't you? But you didn't. You're here in France on your own. And that's awesome!'

Nuala gestured to the croissants and Lindy took one.

'Why I thought buying a crumbling old chateau and doing it up would be an easier option than travelling, I do not know! But I thought it was more practical. Rather than burning through my money simply travelling, I'd be building something for the future.' She gave a hollow laugh. 'Well, I've burned though more money running this place than I could ever have done if I'd travelled round the entire world first class three times!'

'I was just wondering what the running costs would be for a place like this.'

'Don't ask. I naively thought that it might take a few months to do the place up but then I'd be bringing money in with guests and events – maybe even weddings one day. I had such romantic visions.'

'I'm really surprised you're not fully booked. This place is gorgeous,' Nuala told her.

'Well, that's kind of you. I got unlucky with the recent cancellation, but I get good bookings during the summer. Unfortunately, that all evaporates come the end of the season and the online booking platforms I've tried all charge huge commissions. And there've been a few complaints from guests about the weak WiFi and the – well, let's call it the *character* of the place, shall we? Some people are used to luxury and this old place is still a bit rough around the edges. I've tried to be honest with the descriptions online, but people want perfection for their Instagram accounts. And one bad review can do a lot of damage.'

Lindy got up, opened a cabinet and took out a glass before pouring herself an orange juice.

'I hope you don't mind me muscling in on your breakfast.'

'Of course not!' Nuala said. 'I'm enjoying hearing about how you came to be here.'

'I apologise if it's not the rosy picture you imagined. I've not really talked about this to anyone before. The friends I left behind in the States all think it's going swimmingly.'

'Do they visit?'

'They did in the beginning when it was all an adventure, but flights are long and expensive. Same for relatives. We do the Zoom thing, but they don't want to waste precious vacation time on transatlantic flights. I don't blame them.'

'Don't you get lonely out here? What are the locals like?'

'They're all right when I pop into the village. But they're pretty close-knit. I think they were intrigued by a mad American woman buying this old place. I'm sure they must talk about me behind my back. One or two showed an interest. There was an old boy – Pierre; he came and had a look around. Said his grandfather used to take care of the garden here back in the day and he gave me a few tips for what grows well. Not that I've had time to plant anything useful like vegetables. But can you imagine what it would be like?'

Nuala nodded. 'It would be amazing to have a kitchen garden here to feed guests.'

'That's the dream, isn't it? But I've come to realise that dreams cost a lot of money and a place like this needs a lot of people to run it.'

'Do you know of anyone else doing what you're doing? You said you watched all those TV shows. Have you reached out to others?'

'I joined a few online support groups,' Lindy said, 'but

France is a huge country and there isn't anyone near here, and they've all got their own concerns anyway.' She tore into her croissant. 'I had thought there'd be more of a community feel and that we'd all be meeting up to talk about turrets and go antique shopping together, and drinking wine while the sun set.' Lindy shook her head at her own silliness.

'Getting workmen is the other problem. Either you can't find anyone or they take one look at the scale of the job and walk away or give you such a huge quote that they know you won't hire them. I just can't get jobs done. They don't tell you that when you buy the property. And I'm no builder. I'm more the kind of person to come in after the building work and do a little bit of light decorating and design.'

Nuala took one of the croissants, admiring the flakiness of it.

'So what happens next?' Nuala dared to ask.

Lindy took a sip of juice before answering, casting her eyes around the faded grandeur of the dining room as if for the last time. 'I've given it my best shot. I really have. But this place will kill me if I stay here another season.'

'So you're leaving?' Nuala had sensed it was coming but was still saddened to hear it.

'I don't suppose you're looking to buy a chateau?'

Nuala laughed. 'No. I gave up my property in the UK and I'm living in my van.'

'Ah, yes! I remember you talking about that on your YouTube channel. That sounds very sensible to me.'

'Maybe you could trade this place for a van of your own? I can highly recommend it. Well, when they're not broken down in a garage somewhere!'

They smiled at one another.

'You made your dream happen in spite of all the

obstacles,' Lindy said. 'I wish I could say the same.' She sighed. 'Don't get me wrong – it's been magical being here. I lived the dream for a little while and that's what life is all about? What's a life without dreams?'

'Exactly,' Nuala said. 'My dream of travelling around Europe in a van kept me going for those last tough years at work. All those boring hours at a desk or in meetings, I'd nurse it and stoke it – imagining all the places I'd see and the experiences I'd have.'

'And when you left everything behind – how did that feel? I can't imagine not having a home and – well – stuff!'

'It was scary at first,' Nuala admitted. We started slowly sorting out the garage and attic. All those places you don't look at very often so they naturally fill with things you're not that attached to. It helps you build up a kind of minimalist muscle. Letting go of things is very powerful because it makes space not just physically but mentally too.'

Lindy nodded.

'I bought so much stuff for this place. I did all the things a chatelaine is expected to do in these days of consumerism. I bought silver, porcelain, antiques galore! Paintings of horses and long dead aristocrats. I'm going to have to sell it all. Or give it away if nobody wants it. Let's just hope there's another dreamer out there who might be able to get a little bit further with this place than I've been able to.'

'How will you feel leaving it?'

Lindy turned around in her chair and gazed out of one of the windows. 'I'll be a total wreck. For about a week, I imagine!' She laughed. 'But it'll do me no good staying. I'd either work myself into an early grave or die of hyperthermia in the next bad winter we get.' She gave a sigh. 'I'm gonna buy a nice warm farmhouse. There's one here actually but I can't stay so close to the chateau. I couldn't watch someone else living here and making a real go of it when I've failed.'

'But you haven't failed!' Nuala assured her, surprised by her summation.

'No?'

'Think of the adventure you've had. Would you really not want to have experienced that? You'd always be wondering, *what if* if you hadn't done it. Like me with my van trip. I'm anxious a lot of the time and unsure of what I'm doing out here on my own, but I'm so glad I'm doing it because, if I wasn't here, if I'd sold The Van after Paul walked out, I'd be stuck back in the UK always wondering what might have happened if I'd taken a chance.' Nuala smiled. 'We only fail if we give up.'

'But aren't I giving up now?'

'No! You're pivoting having given your dream your best shot. You've ticked that box and decided it wasn't for you after all.'

'Huh!' Lindy nodded. 'You've just saved me years of therapy.'

'And so many people are afraid of failing that they never even begin. That's what I've learned,' Nuala confessed to her. 'I remember talking about this trip to friends and work colleagues and so many of them would tell me that they'd love to do something similar *but*... there was *always* a "but". It's so sad because these limiting beliefs people have stop them from having fun.'

'It was the same when I told people about buying this place,' Lindy told her, taking a couple of grapes from the bowl on the tray and popping them in her mouth. 'There were the doubters, of course. Some people thought I was crazy. But there were a surprising number of people who'd sidle up to me and tell me of similar dreams. It might not be a French chateau – it might be a dream of having a cabin by a lake or a place in the mountains somewhere. I'd recognise that look in their eyes – that dreamer's look, you know?'

'Oh, yes!'

'And I'd think, well why aren't you going to at least *try* and make it happen?'

'It's crazy, isn't it?' Nuala said. 'We get just one crack at this thing called life and I want to give it the very best shot I've got.'

'Exactly!' Lindy said, stealing a couple more grapes. 'Listen – I'll let you get on with your breakfast before I eat any more of it.'

'Didn't you say you wanted my help with some painting?' Nuala asked, pouring another cup of tea as Lindy got up to go.

'Only if you're up for it. The west turret bedroom could definitely use a couple of coats before I show prospective buyers around.'

Nuala grinned and Lindy left the room.

After finishing her breakfast, Nuala got changed into a spare pair of decorator's overalls that Lindy had. Nu thought about the conversation she'd had with Lindy and how wonderful it was to meet such a determined woman who'd had a dream and had crossed an ocean to a foreign country to make it come true.

Sitting in the window seat and gazing down into the overgrown gardens, she let the romance of the chateau wash over her for a moment. It was very hard not to fall in love with such a place even when you knew of all the pitfalls. That's why these places kept selling. Dreamers will always dream.

Nuala wondered what it might be like to be the owner of such a place. A *chatelaine*! She had a European passport courtesy of her Irish family so she could actually move to France if she so chose. What would that be like, she wondered. To leave the UK behind and start a new life in a new country? The thought was a seductive one. It would certainly help to put some permanent distance between her and her past.

But she didn't want to buy another property and start accumulating things again and she certainly didn't have the budget for a chateau. She wanted her freedom – for now. But who knew how she'd feel about the prospect of buying a property in the future like the modest farmhouse Lindy was now looking for? Wasn't that one of the miracles of life – to evolve, change your mind and develop new ideas and passions? And it certainly made Nuala aware of the endless options that were available to her which was incredibly exciting. Just a few weeks ago, she'd never have imagined having the courage or will to travel solo in The Van and yet here she was loving her freedom. She didn't know how long this adventure would last. When she'd been planning it with Paul, they'd said they'd take their time. Nuala had always imagined at least five years and maybe much longer. That's why they'd invested in a brand-new vehicle – it was to be their home for the foreseeable future. It sometimes scared Nuala when she thought about that. How long would she be able to keep this dream of hers going now that she was living it on her own? Perhaps the dream might even change. Maybe she'd find a place she'd want to stay.

The joy of it was that she could make up her own rules. The future was wide open to her. She only had to look, be inspired and have the courage to go for it.

CHAPTER TWENTY-ONE

Elise watched as Julia moved around the tiny Puglian kitchen with such grace and patience. Nothing seemed to faze her – not the three pans on the cooker nor the many different herbs that lay waiting for preparation that had come straight from the garden just minutes before. She looked totally at ease. Totally at home.

'I used to have one of those big white and silver kitchens with all the gadgets and the soft-close drawers. The taps with still and sparkling water. Everything you could ever imagine wanting.' Julia shook her head. 'And I didn't want it! But this – this old place with its ill-fitting drawers and years of wear – I can relax here. I can fling things about and not be precious, you know?'

Elise nodded, immediately understanding the sentiment.

'You have to be relaxed if you're going to cook a good meal. I think so anyway. I always felt so – so *rigid* – in that all mod cons kitchen. It was Nick's idea – my ex-husband. He wanted the latest, flashiest kitchen. Only he never cooked in it. He'd only ever make coffee in this horribly noisy machine he insisted on having – the one that does all the fancy froth. What a waste of energy!'

Elise couldn't help laughing at that.

'But here – I can splatter tomato sauce up the walls and not worry. It's wonderful!'

'Do you ever go back to the UK?'

'I did just once to sort out the divorce. I only have one sister and she comes here. I can't bear to go back now. My life is here.' She smiled. 'No looking back!'

'So tell me how you came to be here.'

'Ah, yes! I'm being all mysterious, aren't I? And I promised to tell you everything.'

It was then that one of the pans started to boil over.

'I'll tell you what – let's have dinner first!'

And what a splendid dinner it was. Julia had made the pasta herself and the sauce was the best Elise had ever tasted. The wine Julia's husband Marco poured was a local one. He did his best to explain the ingredients, but Elise couldn't understand all the Italian words and, when he attempted to say them in English, his accent was so thick that it didn't really shed any more light.

When he excused himself to leave the ladies to their conversation, Julia smiled after him.

'His mother still disapproves of us,' she confessed, 'but I think I'll win her round eventually.'

'Why doesn't she approve?'

'You know – divorced older English woman. I'm the wrong side of forty now.'

'But Marco's older than you!'

'I know. I think Gianna still imagined he'd find some young Italian woman who'd give her lots of grandchildren.'

'So he has no family?'

'No. He told me he was wed to the land. Until he met me.' Julia allowed herself a smile of satisfaction at that. 'He said he never thought he'd meet anyone who'd want to live in the middle of nowhere with him. Oh, how wrong he was!'

'And you *are* going to tell me how you came to be in the middle of nowhere with him, aren't you?' Elise pressed, taking a sip of her wine and determining to buy several bottles to have shipped home.

Julia sighed. 'I haven't thought about that summer for some time now. Isn't that funny? And it seems like a lifetime ago.' She drained her wine glass and refilled it, offering Elise a top-up which she happily accepted.

'It had been a stressful year. My husband, Nick, had got a recent promotion and was working even longer hours than normal. Not that he minded. He thrived on that kind of thing. And, to be honest, I didn't mind either. We'd been spending less time together over the preceding months and I was finding it was something of a relief. Is that awful to admit? Anyway, it came time to book our summer holiday. Nick usually left that up to me, but carefully directed my searches with suggestions of all the places he'd seen on social media. You know the sort? All those ghastly destinations with perfect manicured beaches and infinity pools.' She laughed.

'I guess I'd been spoilt over the years. Nick's salary had allowed us to stay in some of the most glamorous locations in the world but they always felt a bit empty to me. I liked the rougher places. Not that this is exactly roughing it. But do you know what I mean? Puglia – it seemed like I'd find something of the *real* Italy here so, rather than booking the perfect villa overlooking the Amalfi coast or something way too expensive in Rome or Tuscany, I found this place.'

She paused to sip her wine.

'And how did Nick react?' Elise asked.

'He was furious,' Julia admitted. 'He actually demanded that I cancel it, but I said it was non-refundable and he hates losing money. I showed him we'd be staying in a trullo but he didn't seem overly impressed. Honestly, he was more concerned about other people's reactions to his holiday photos than how his wife would feel while actually on holiday. He was such a snob that way. But I truly – *trulli* – thought he'd fall in love with it all once we were actually here. You know – see its charm and fall under its spell.'

'It would be hard not to,' Elise said, thinking of how adorable the trullo was.

Julia shrugged. 'He never said a word. Can you believe it? He was on the phone virtually the whole time. One day, I hid it and he went crazy tearing the whole place apart. "I've got a call coming in. I've got a call coming in," he kept chanting. Well, he *always* had a call coming in. We kind of became stranded here because he kept right on working. And that was okay to begin with as it was peaceful and I swam and read and sunbathed. But we only went into Alberobello in the evenings once office hours were done.'

'Did you tell him how you felt?'

'Oh, yes. I kept telling him about all the amazing places there were to see in the area, but he just said that we'd go out later. Later. Later. It was always "later" with Nick.'

'So I took myself for walks. There are quite a few footpaths around here – some a bit rougher than others – but all with wonderful views and it felt good to be walking and seeing something of the Puglian landscape. I started taking photos and looking forward to my time on my own and then, one day, I saw a man working in one of the olive groves. He was a bit older than me and looked like he'd spent his entire life outdoors. His skin was so tanned and he had a big dark beard and was wearing this old checked shirt with a great hole in it. I took a few photos of him and he spotted me. I tried to flee but he called me over. I was so embarrassed but it turned out that the trullo we were staying in belonged to him. We hadn't met the owner. We'd simply let ourselves in using a key safe. He explained his English wasn't very good but it was certainly better than my Italian and we managed to chat. Honestly, I think we talked more that day – in our broken way – than I had with my husband on the holiday until that point.'

'I met him the next day and asked if I could photograph him as he worked. He thought it was funny that anyone should want to take pictures of him but, when I showed them to him, he seemed pleased. And he looked so at home in the landscape – like he'd grown right up out of the earth alongside his beloved olive trees.'

'He does have that look about him,' Elise agreed.

Julia nodded. 'And such a contrast to Nick in his white shirts with his white skin due to being stuck indoors on his phone or laptop all day.

'But the real difference wasn't physical – it was emotional. Because Marco would listen to me, and I'm not even sure how much he understood as his English is quite limited, but he really *seemed* to be listening, you know? His *eyes* were listening.' Julia gave a little laugh. 'His body. His whole being. He paid me the sort of attention that Nick never had. Or at least not in the last few years of our marriage.'

She looked wistful at that and Elise wasn't quite sure how to respond.

'You know, Nick actually set up an office in the kitchen at the trullo?' Julia went on. 'He'd brought his laptop with him and had everything set up so we couldn't use the table for a proper breakfast.'

'That's not ideal, is it?'

'Anyway, I spent more and more time with Marco.'

'And Nick didn't get suspicious?'

'No! He just thought I'd taken up walking and photography. He actually encouraged it. "It's doing you good," he told me one morning as I was getting ready to leave. "Take your time. I've got a call coming in." So I took my time – with Marco.'

She smiled and Elise couldn't help wondering exactly what had been going on in that olive grove that summer.

'You know when you find the place where you belong?' Julia asked with a wistful smile.

Elise nodded but felt a little guilty because she'd never truly experienced that for herself. Not unless she counted her office at work and that wasn't so much about belonging as making the very best out of circumstances.

'Well, I felt that as soon as I saw this farmhouse,' Julia went on. 'It was run-down and ramshackle. Its paint was flakey and its shutters were skew-whiff but it just seemed so welcoming. It was so very different from the homes I'd had with Nick – the architect-designed barn conversions and expensive loft flats. This was full of old comfy furniture that had been inherited, and been slept on by dogs for decades. It felt loved and lived in. And, when Marco invited me in, he didn't make any pretence about it. He didn't straighten anything or try to hide things – he just led me into this kitchen and opened a bottle of wine.'

Elise nodded. 'He gets his priorities right!'

'Exactly!'

'And Nick had no idea you were with Marco during the day?'

'None at all. I'm not sure what he imagined I was doing for hours on end. I mean, there are only so many ways you can photograph trulli and tracks, aren't there?'

'Did he ask to look at your photos?'

'I showed him a few choice ones just to give me an alibi,' Julia confessed. 'I didn't show him the ones of Marco though.' She laughed.

'So what happened next?' Elise asked, keen to move the story along.

'Well, one morning towards the end of our fortnight at the trullo, Nick woke up and said, "Let's go somewhere!"'

'I was so surprised but he seemed to want to make things up to me. Said it had been crazy busy in the office during his absence but that he was completely mine for the day. The trouble was, I didn't really want him. Not for a whole day. But what could I do? I quickly ran up to the farmhouse while Nick was in the shower but Marco wasn't around so I left him a note. I hated not being able to see him. It's amazing how quickly we get used to a new routine, isn't it? Anyway, Nick and I drove to Monopoli on the coast. It's a beautiful city. He took me to some fancy restaurant and we walked along the harbour and took a little boat trip. And you know what? It was nice. He only glanced at his phone a couple of times but I could see he was making an effort. He even apologised for his behaviour. It was...' She paused. 'A glimpse at what our life could be like.'

'So what happened?'

'The next day was exactly the same as the all the others before our trip out, with Nick on his phone and laptop. And then it came to our final day. We were taking an evening flight home but we had to get to the airport by mid-afternoon so we spent the morning at the trullo. I swam and went for a walk. I told Marco it was time to leave and he...' She paused for a moment and Elise felt her breath catch in her throat, 'he took my face in his hands and they were warm and rough with farm work – like the bark of one of his olive trees – and he whispered something to me. Something in Italian that I didn't quite understand. At least, not in words. But I felt it.'

'When I got back to the trullo, Nick had packed. He was texting somebody and I looked at the car boot open for my suitcase. He nodded towards it and I went inside to finish packing.'

'When I came outside, he was at the back of the car. His face was still as white as when we'd first arrived. He'd hardly seen the sunshine and had only seen one solitary city. I was so cross with him.'

'"Come on, darling! We don't want a fine for returning this car late, do we?" he said. He didn't even look at me as he was talking. He was still texting. That kind of made up my mind. Although, if I'm being absolutely honest, I'd already made it up.'

'"I'm not coming." I told him. "I'm staying."'

'"Staying where?" he asked.'

'"Here. Well, not *here*. At the farmhouse."'

'He got a bit fractious then. Asking me what the hell was I talking about. He really wasn't listening to me so I walked towards him and put my hand over his phone. Only then did he look at me properly.' She paused again and Elise shifted forward in her chair.

'"Listen to me",' I told him. "I'm staying here. I've met someone and I'm leaving you."'

Elise gasped at Julia's boldness.

'What did he say?'

Julia shrugged. 'You know what? I really can't remember his exact words because my head was so full of Marco and my new life. I think I'd tuned out of my marriage some time before. There'd been little glimmers of hope, of course. A twenty-year-old marriage can't be discarded lightly. Anyway, I just remember that we had an almighty row and I didn't feel any of Nick's love for me. He showed no real emotion other than anger. He was probably just panicking at the thought of what he'd say to his family and work colleagues. He's probably told them I died. I don't know. That would make it easier for him to save face.'

'And he left you here?'

'When it became clear he'd miss the plane home if he didn't go – yes!'

'Did you leave a job back in the UK?'

'I gave my job up when I married Nick. It was a really old-fashioned arrangement, but I didn't mind in the beginning. He was the earner and I was the housewife. We'd always expected to have children, you see, only that never happened. So I filled my days with charity work. I guess I was lucky to be able to do that and I miss it. I don't miss the politics of it all, mind. Some of those charities are run by real harridans.' She laughed. 'Whereas life here is so easy. It's real. It's from the earth. We spend so much time outdoors and I love that. You forget how vital that is when you live in the UK. We're all so bundled up in warm clothes with the central heating on. We live in stifling rooms with unnatural lights.'

Elise nodded and it was then that Marco came back in

with a new bottle of wine and smiled at Julia. Elise could see the radiance in that smile and his total absorption with her.

'You have a good life here,' Elise told them both as Marco poured the wine.

He smiled and nodded, accepting the simple fact that Elise was right.

'I call this chapter of my life "Julia in Puglia",' Julia said.

Elise laughed.

'Will there be more chapters?'

'Who knows?' she said. 'Only they will all be with Marco, God willing.'

Elise watched as he bent to kiss Julia and her heart swelled with joy at the scene.

'Life can be messy and unpredictable,' Julia went on, 'but it can also be so surprisingly wonderful. When I came here, I had absolutely no idea that it would become my home. I didn't plan that and I certainly didn't have any weird premonitions when I saw the trullo online and booked it. Don't you just love that? You never know when your whole life will do a complete one-eighty.'

Elise nodded. It was both a marvellous and terrifying thought. The best often were.

Marco offered to drive Elise back to the trullo but she wanted to walk. There was a waxing gibbous moon and she wanted to experience the full beauty of the Puglian countryside. No traffic, no light pollution and nobody else around. As she set off, it did cross her mind that there could be wildlife. Were there wild boar in this part of Italy? Or wolves even? Should she have asked? Surely Julia and Marco would have insisted on taking her back to the trullo if they deemed it unsafe for her to go on foot alone.

She mulled over Julia's story. How inspiring it had been

to hear of her break from the life that had been holding her prisoner for so long. To know that escape was always possible even when we weren't looking for it and that other lives could be led if you allowed yourself the time and space to find them. Elise wondered just how many lives were possible for one person and why she had limited herself so much over the years living that tiny life in the Midlands town. What might have happened if she'd dared to break away? If she'd taken a trip or two over the years? If she'd said "no" to her mother more often and "yes" to life instead? Who might she have become? Where might she have been living? Or was life turning out just the way it was meant to and she wasn't ever meant to feel all this until this very moment?

As she gazed through the olive groves up towards the moon, she realised that she didn't have the answers to any of her questions. But she was grateful that she was at least asking them.

She wasn't quite ready for sleep when she got back to the trullo so she picked up the beautiful marbled notebook she'd bought in Florence. She felt so inspired by Julia's story of how she'd had the courage to change her life when the opportunity presented itself to her. What might that actually be like, Elise couldn't help wondering. To meet somebody. To fall in love.

She thought about the way Julia lit up when she spoke about Marco - the light in her eyes, the curve of her smile — even her hair seemed to bounce when she talked about him. Elise couldn't begin to imagine what that might feel like. To respond to someone with your whole being. It must be truly intoxicating and she couldn't help wanting to experience that because she believed she never really had. Surely she'd know if she had. On the plus side, she'd never had her heart broken by a man, but didn't they say it was better to have loved and lost than never to have loved at all?

What do you want, Elise?

The voice inside her was strong tonight – willing her to explore and examine, to dream and demand.

And so she wrote in her notebook, the words pouring from her heart onto the creamy Florentine pages as the moon softly glowed in the Puglian sky. She wrote about wanting to feel things – *really* feel things! To experience love, to meet someone and know what it was to feel truly connected to another person. Whether for a day or a month. Or a lifetime.

CHAPTER TWENTY-TWO

The day trip to La Gomera ended all too soon. Laurie had just about got used to being on the back of a motorbike again and she'd loved seeing the dramatic landscape of the island from that vantage point. And, yes, she had also enjoyed the attention of a handsome young man. There hadn't been time to do anything but see a few sights in the brief window before heading back to the island's capital, San Sebastián, in time for the ferry. It was fascinating for Laurie to accompany Santi on board as he parked his bike, securing it with a strap like a pro. They took off their protective clothing and then made their way to the bar before the crowds from the coaches got there. Santi bought coffee for them both.

'This is disgusting!' he complained as he took his first sip. 'When we get back, I'll take you to a place for a proper coffee – Tenerife style!'

She smiled. She loved the way he said Tenerife – the proper Spanish way: Teneri*fay*.

They didn't want to sit indoors so, after finishing their

coffees, they made their way to the back of the boat, letting the wind blow in their hair as the boat left the harbour and crossed the sea between the two Canarian islands. Laurie felt a little chilly in her light dress and cotton cardigan, but also exhilarated. She was just enormously grateful for the afternoon she'd had with Santi. She'd never imagined that she'd have such an adventure and she could feel that she was still carrying a huge bubble of excitement inside her.

She glanced at Santi as he stood next to her at the rail, his eyes fixed on the horizon, the sea spray on his tanned face and his dark hair blowing back. He was so handsome.

And so young!

Young enough to be your son.

But, rather crucially, he *wasn't* her son. He was a good-looking young man who seemed to have taken a shine to her. Was it appropriate? Who was she to question him? It was harmless enough, wasn't it? A little bit of flirtatious fun on a sunny island. The climate seemed to demand such behaviour and it would be a shame if she didn't relax a little and enjoy what she was being offered.

Take this very moment, she thought. She was hyper aware of how close they were standing to each other as they watched the magical island of La Gomera disappearing from view beyond the wild wake of white water. Laurie half-expected Santi to disappear too, but he stayed with her, resting his hand on hers on the cold metal railing.

'It's a shame we didn't get longer in San Sebastián,' she said to Santi, raising her voice to be heard above the wind. 'I hope I didn't miss anything. I don't feel I saw much of the culture of the island although we were treated to a whistling demonstration at lunch.'

'Ah, *el silbo*? The famous language of the mountains?'

'Yes. It's fascinating. Do you know much about it?'

'Not really. There's a museum in the capital, but it's probably just full of photos of people whistling.'

Laurie laughed at his summation and watched as he turned his attention back to the horizon. What was he thinking, she couldn't help wondering. And what was going to happen next? He'd said he'd take her for coffee. But would she really go with him? Wouldn't it be better to end things once they reached the port at Los Cristianos? It had been such a day of fun. They'd enjoyed each other's company and she had nothing to feel guilty about. As far as Laurie could see, there would be no harm in going for coffee with him.

She might have known that she wouldn't get off the ferry scot-free. Having followed Santi back down to his bike, she was starting to pull on the leather trousers he'd lent her when she saw the tour guide from her coach trip watching her. Antonio did an almost comical double take and a huge smile stretched across his face – almost as big as the blush that crossed Laurie's. Once again, she cursed the bright dress she was wearing which must have drawn his eye to her. Then again, wasn't it the dress – at least in part – that had caught Santi's eye and had led to this wonderful adventure today? Anyway, why was she worried what the tour guide might be thinking? But, of course, she did worry and her imagination immediately leapt to her being judged by the young man for – well – being in the company of a *young man*.

Laurie decided to brazen it out and gave a little wave. The tour guide waved back.

'Who's that?' Santi asked. 'Another young man of yours, huh?'

Laurie gave him a wry smile and finished putting the leather trousers and jacket back on for the ride into town.

A few minutes later, they'd parked the bike and got changed again before Santi led her through the backstreets, arriving at a bar a few minutes later. The Purple Turtle. It looked quirky and fun and it was certainly a popular place, but they managed to find a small table at the back. They ordered some tapas and Santi got a soda and ordered something called a *barraquito* for Laurie.

'It's a kind of coffee cocktail,' he told her. 'You'll love it!'

'Aren't you having one?'

He shook his head and she wondered briefly if he might be trying to get her tipsy, but the curious thing was that she didn't really mind. It had been years, *decades*, since she'd been tipsy – let alone had a man want to make her feel tipsy – to soften the edges of her life and give her the sweet gift of mellowness.

When the *barraquito* arrived along with the tapas, Laurie gasped. It was unlike anything she had ever seen before. It came in a tall, slender glass with a handle and was in several very distinct layers.

'Condensed milk, liqueur, espresso and a little lemon and cinnamon,' Santi explained. 'It's very Canarian. Very *Tenerife!*'

'It's lovely!' Laurie told him as she examined the pretty colours of the drink and couldn't help thinking that it was basically flirtation in a glass. But it touched her that he wanted to share something local with her.

She got her phone out and took a photo.

'Oh, you're one of those who takes pictures of everything they eat and drink?' Santi teased.

'No! I just want to remember it. It's so pretty!'

'Are you going to try it or just look at it?'

Laurie smiled and picked up the glass.

'Stir it first!'

'Oh, right!'

Laurie picked up the long metal spoon from the saucer and stirred the drink, swirling the pretty layers together until the creams, yellow and deep espresso colours mixed and blended into the most perfect coffee shade. Only then did she take her first sip.

Santi was watching her – his deep brown eyes attentive.

Laurie licked her lips. 'It's good. Very... smooth, but with a kick. It definitely has heat.'

'The best things in life always do,' Santi whispered.

Laurie could feel herself blushing. 'Do you want a sip?'

He shook his head. 'No. I want to watch you drink it all.'

As she raised the glass to her lips again, Laurie couldn't help feeling a little self-conscious. She couldn't remember the last time she'd felt so closely observed.

She cleared her throat. 'So do you have travel plans beyond Tenerife?'

He popped one of the tapas bites into his mouth and shrugged. 'I don't like to plan too far ahead. But mainland Spain, I think. Seville before it gets too hot in the summer. Have you been?'

'No,' Laurie said, thinking of Kitty from the yoga retreat who was there now and how much she longed to see the city too.

'Ah, Laurie! It's the most beautiful city in the world! The old town is full of crazy little streets and bars. Music everywhere. Flamenco too. You would love it!'

'And then where?'

'Maybe Granada or further south. Marrakesh perhaps. Or Istanbul. I don't know. I'll see how I feel. I like to see in the moment, you know?'

She nodded. She was beginning to feel the power of the present moment so much more these days and it was highly intoxicating.

'But it'll be fun – wherever I go. The world should be enjoyed, right?'

'Right!'

'I want to see things – beautiful places. I want to eat the food the locals eat. I want to wake up and not remember where I am.' He laughed.

'I love that.'

'What?' he asked. 'What do you love?'

'The way you see the world – it's like a big playground for you.'

'Sure. Why not?' He caught her hand across the table. 'You should come with me, Laurie!'

'What?'

'Imagine the fun we could have!'

'Oh, Santi! I don't think–'

'We had a good time today, *si*?'

'*Si!* Yes. Of course.'

'That doesn't need to end, does it? You want to see places. I want to see places. Why not together?'

His eyes were so intense now. Oh, how easy it would be to fall for him, she thought.

'Look!' she said suddenly uneasy and withdrawing her hand from his. 'I'm not sure what's going on here.'

Santi looked confused. 'What do you mean?'

'I mean you and me.'

'We're living! We're... we're... having fun, no?'

'Yes,' she said guardedly.

'Then what's the problem?'

She took a deep breath. 'You do know I'm fifty-two, don't you?'

'Sure. So what?'

'I could be your mother, Santi!'

He frowned at that and then he leaned a little closer to her. 'But you're not,' he told her, echoing her own thoughts from before.

'I'm on HRT,' she retorted.

'I don't know what that is.'

'I'm wearing a patch on my bottom.'

'You can show me later,' he countered without missing a beat.

Laurie burst out laughing.

'I'll order you another drink, yes?' he said.

'Yes! I mean – *no!*'

'No?'

They locked eyes and, almost without thinking, Laurie picked her spoon up and started to stir her drink again. She had to remain in control here. She was the adult in this situation and she had to behave like one. Besides, she was a married woman. The trouble was, she hadn't *felt* married in such a long time. She hadn't felt anything much. Until now. Until this moment with Santi.

'I think I'd better get back to my hotel.'

'No, Laurie – it's so early.'

'It's been a long day.'

'Are you tired?' he asked.

She considered the question carefully before answering it. If she said she was tired, she'd sound so old and boring and she didn't want to sound like that. She didn't want to *be* that. And the truth was she wasn't actually feeling tired. She could feel the thrum of the alcohol and espresso in her body and it felt wonderful. But what was even more wonderful was the attention Santi was paying her. That was the real drug here.

'I should go back,' she heard herself saying.

Santi sighed. 'Okay. I'll walk you back.'

'What about your bike?'

'I'll get it later. It's not far.'

'You don't need to walk with me, Santi.'

'Hey – I'm a gentleman!'

She smiled and he returned the smile.

After finishing their drinks and tapas, they left The Purple Turtle just as a crowd of young people was arriving. There were three beautiful young women amongst them and Laurie watched Santi to see if he'd pay them any attention, but he didn't. Instead, he took her hand in his and they walked side by side so easily and naturally it was as if they were already a couple.

They didn't talk much on the way to Laurie's hotel. Santi pointed out a few sights: another bar that he liked and a restaurant Laurie should most definitely avoid. He grimaced at the tourist tat sold in all the shops – the gaudy towels and the silly hats, and Laurie found herself apologising for her fellow Brits who lapped it all up.

'You mustn't be snobbish, Santi. You have the sunshine in your country and we don't.'

'But look at the ugly things. And the English food everywhere. Why do you come here and eat English food? I don't understand!'

'But I've just eaten tapas and had a *barraquito*,' she told him.

'Yes. That's because you're special.'

A warmth spread through her – swift and unsettling.

They walked on.

'Well, here we are,' she said a few minutes later.

'Ah, yes – your ugly hotel.'

'Yes.'

'You shouldn't stay here. You should have a more... *authentic* experience.'

She smiled. 'Perhaps.'

'I stay in a friend's place. He's away. I – how do you say?'

'Housesit?'

'Yes. One week more. He has a cat. Do you like cats?'

She nodded. 'I do.'

'Then you would love Nura! She's like a cloud. And the house.'

'Is like a cloud?'

'No!' He laughed. 'It's a proper Canarian house with wooden shutters and a balcony. You should see it.'

'You think so?'

'Yes. I think so.' He smiled that charming smile which very nearly undid her. 'Let me show it to you.' He leaned closer so that his breath was warm on her face. 'I think you will love it, Laurie.'

She gazed into his brown eyes which looked so earnest now and much less boyish. And then she looked up at the huge bulk of the hotel where she was staying and thought about the grim room with the atrocious soundproofing, the lack of air conditioning, and – perhaps most importantly – the woman she'd been when she'd first checked in. That woman wouldn't have spent the day with Santi. She wouldn't have jumped on to the back of a bike or smiled the way she'd smiled today.

She looked back at Santi. This was dangerous, she couldn't help thinking. But it was also rather thrilling because there was a definite spark between them and she knew that she didn't want to extinguish it.

END OF BOOK ONE

Margaret, Victoria's great grandmother - inspiration for Clara Beech.

ACKNOWLEDGEMENTS

As ever, huge thanks to my brilliant team: Catri, Jane and Roy. I couldn't do any of this without you all!

And thank you to Lyn for the beautiful photograph of Margaret.

ABOUT THE AUTHOR

Victoria Connelly is the bestselling author of *The Rose Girls* and *The Beauty of Broken Things*.

With over a million sales, her books have been translated into a dozen languages. The first, *Flights of Angels*, was made into a film in Germany. Victoria flew to Berlin to see it being made and even played a cameo role in it.

A Weekend with Mr Darcy, the first in her popular Austen Addicts series about fans of Jane Austen has sold over 100,000 copies. She is also the author of several romantic comedies including *The Runaway Actress* which was nominated for the Romantic Novelists' Association's Best Romantic Comedy of the Year.

Victoria was brought up in Norfolk, England before

moving to Yorkshire where she got married in a medieval castle. After 11 years in London, she moved to rural Suffolk where she lives in a pink thatched cottage with her artist husband, a springer spaniel and her ex-battery hens. She's passionate about solo travel and loves making short films about the places she visits for her YouTube channel: @EnglishWriterExplores

To hear about future releases and receive a **free ebook** sign up for her newsletter at www.victoriaconnelly.com.

ALSO BY VICTORIA CONNELLY

The House in the Clouds Series

The House in the Clouds

High Blue Sky

The Colour of Summer

The Book Lovers Series

The Book Lovers

Rules for a Successful Book Club

Natural Born Readers

Scenes from a Country Bookshop

Christmas with the Book Lovers

One More Page Before I Kiss You

Other Books

The Way to the Sea

The Beauty of Broken Things

One Last Summer

The Heart of the Garden

Love in an English Garden

The Rose Girls

The Secret of You

Christmas at The Cove

Christmas at the Castle

Christmas at the Cottage

The Wrong Ghost

The Christmas Collection - Volumes One and Two

A Summer to Remember

Wish You Were Here

The Runaway Actress

Molly's Millions

A Weekend with Mr Darcy

The Perfect Hero (Dreaming of Mr Darcy)

Mr Darcy Forever

Christmas With Mr Darcy

Happy Birthday Mr Darcy

At Home with Mr Darcy

Escape to Mulberry Cottage (non-fiction)

A Year at Mulberry Cottage (non-fiction)

Summer at Mulberry Cottage (non-fiction)

Finding Old Thatch (non-fiction)

The Garden at Old Thatch (non-fiction)

Introvert Abroad

Introvert Explores

VICTORIA CONNELLY

FAMILY PORTRAIT

Sometimes, it's those closest to you who are hiding the most.

After the death of their artist father, Alex, Brenna and Cordelia Bellwood return to Slate House – the Victorian mansion in the Lake District where they grew up together. But the three siblings have very different memories of being there and of their relationship with their famous father.

For Alex, his passion for art was always overshadowed by his father's fame. For Brenna, life was turned upside down when their mother left them, forcing her to grow up much too quickly. And Cordelia – once the beloved muse of her father – now questions her role after a shocking revelation that threatens the whole family.

Set against the beautiful backdrop of Grasmere, Family Portrait is a lyrical and poignant story showing that the things that tear us apart can also bring us together again.

MILLION SELLING AUTHOR
Victoria Connelly
Introvert Explores
Europe
&
Beyond
Exploring the world
one fear at a time.

After a year of tentative travel, author Victoria Connelly is ready for something a little more adventurous… and this time, she's going solo!

Warming up with some winter sunshine in Tenerife, she then joins a group tour through the wonders of Turkey, then straps on a backpack for a journey through Austria, Slovakia, and Hungary – braving her first hostel stay in over thirty years. Next stop: northern Italy by train – calling at Bologna, Florence, Padua, and Verona.

Four solo trips. One unforgettable year.

Join anxious adventurer Victoria as she slowly builds confidence, embraces the unknown, and uncovers a version of herself she never knew existed. From paragliding in the Canaries to haggling in the bazaars of Istanbul, this is a heartwarming tale of courage, discovery, and the quiet joy of becoming your own best companion.

Packed with colour photos, Introvert Explores is a love letter to bravery, reinvention, and the transformative power of travel.